LUNA STATION
QUARTERLY

Issue 036 | December 2018

Editor-in-Chief
Jennifer Lyn Parsons

Editors
Linda Codega • Caroljean Gavin
Shel Graves • Cathrin Hagey • Dana Mele
Kimberly Osgood • Gô Shoemake

LUNA STATION PRESS
NEW JERSEY

First Paperback Edition December 2018
ISBN: 978-1-949077-02-5

Luna Station Quarterly publishes short fiction on March 1st, June 1st,
September 1st, and December 1st. For more information and submission
guidelines, please visit our website at lunastationquarterly.com

LUNA STATION PRESS

For Luna Station Press

Creative Director - Tara Quinn Lindsey
Editor-in-Chief & Founder - Jennifer Lyn Parsons

www.lunastationpress.com

CONTENTS

Editorial

Tara Quinn Lindsey

Tara Quinn Lindsey is a poet & essayist. Her books include *The Esbat Sequence, sQuallor//gLamour, Invisible Compositions* & *Bedtime Stories For Insouciant Alchemists*. To learn more, visit her at taralindsey.com

"Hard times are coming, when we'll be wanting the voices of writers who can see alternatives to how we live now, can see through our fear-stricken society and its obsessive technologies to other ways of being, and even imagine real grounds for hope. We'll need writers who can remember freedom—poets, visionaries—realists of a larger reality..." - Ursula K. Le Guin

Hi everyone! Allow me to introduce myself. My name is Tara Quinn Lindsey, and I am the Creative Director of Luna Station Press. This is a fancy way of saying that I normally write the back cover copy description for each issue, and that I am a combination of Cyrano de Bergerac and an Oblique Strategy to our beloved Editor In Chief, Jennifer Parsons. (Those are good references, gang...look 'em up!) It's also a fancy way of saying that I have the honour and privilege of being the first person other than JP in the nine year history of The Quarterly to write this editorial, as I have finally convinced her to put one of her stories in the magazine she founded. Fair minded soul that she is, she didn't want to have two pieces in one issue, so here we are.

I've known about this special Crone issue for well over a year, and have been waiting impatiently for it to manifest. It is, in fact, the first of what will now be an annual tradition for The

Quarterly, that our Winter issue will be a themed one. What an interesting and exciting change, to give our writers such a deep and abiding archetype to play with, and then see all the different flavors of story that spring from this one well!

Who is she, then? Sometimes Goddess, sometimes mortal, she is the third verse in the original trinity of Maiden, Mother & Crone, seen in countless variations and under different names around the world. She has wisdom and experience to spare. She is kind and she is frightening. Sometimes she is an aspect of The One Who Is Three. Sometimes she is simply your mother or grandmother or favorite neighbor. Whatever the case, you know her. You've always known her. And if you're lucky, one day you may become her. For all I know, you may be her already...

When I started thinking about how to crack this editorial, it hit me that I've been personally unlucky with regard to influential Crone figures. I have no older female relatives or neighbors or teachers, and I myself am squarely in the Mother years, though I am intentionally child free. So where to look? Surely I could go on for a bit about some of the Wise Old Ones of my acquaintance, the Calliach and Baba Yaga and the like. But in the interest of making this a bit more universal, and since this is going in a literary magazine, I think a few words about a Crone or two of the creative/literary variety is the way to go.

Nearly four years ago now, on December 30th, 2014, I had the incredible pleasure and privilege of attending Patti Smith's 68th birthday concert at Webster Hall in New York City. Sure, you've probably heard of her, at least if you are of a certain age. You may have a copy of Horses laying around, or sing along to Because The Night when it comes on classic rock radio. But have you read Just Kids? Have you listened to Gone Again? If you have, you may have an idea of what I experienced that night, standing right in front of the stage (my reward for standing in line since 530pm) seeing and hearing an authentic, deeply sincere Wise Woman dig deep, honouring her past while aging ferociously and without apology. Seek her out, especially if you've never heard of her. Seriously, you have no idea...

I can't imagine I have to give a primer to readers of this fine publication on the merits and talents of the legendary, late Ursula K. Le Guin. Many of us, i'm sure, have read Left Hand of Darkness or the Earthsea books (or my personal favorite, Always Coming Home) but when considering the Crone, it's hard to do better than to spend time with Ursula's lesser known, late period poetry and non-fiction collections. Maybe you saw No Time To Spare on a featured table after she died. Follow that up with Words Are My Matter (which features the "Freedom" speech that the quote above comes from) or her poetry collections Late In The Day and So Far So Good. And don't even get me started on how quietly life changing her Tao Te Ching interpretation is...

I could go on, but I know you're excited to get to these stories. They are some of the finest we have ever published. As I take my leave, a heartfelt thank you to JP for this opportunity to say a few words on a topic dear to my heart, to our incredible staff and authors for making Luna Station the amazing egregore that it is, and of course to our readers, without whom...

Happy reading, and if you encounter Her, be sure to give the Calliach Her due.

L S Q | 036

One of the little ones
called me Calliach today
as I put my puppets

away, as I counted
the years since I last
visited the floating forest

I didn't think anyone
remembered the
old gods

anymore

-Quinn, of Thorn

Butterflies

Elizabeth Hinckley

As a naturalist and an author, Elizabeth Hinckley has a passion for both the natural world and the power of story, and their ability to inspire the human spirit. She is the author of David, A Rat. She lives in New Jersey, home to a surprisingly beautiful and diverse array of natural wonders, which she explores frequently.

Before the insects died, people at large did not care what I did for a living, and in many ways, I did not care what they did, so long as they left me alone. After the insects died, people might have looked to me for answers, if they had understood that it all started with them. The irony is that, after they were gone, what would they have expected me to do? Anything of value I had to offer would have been in warning, and best heeded before it all went to hell. In any case, people didn't look to me for anything of the sort. They wanted a mother, which was just the sort of woman I had decided not to be after all.

I was an entomologist, doing field research on insects and living for long periods of time in field stations, tents, and cabins, more often than not feeling antagonistic towards people, whose shortsightedness was causing irreparable damage to the world. Habitats were shrinking, weather was wilding, and species disappearing. Back then, we still thought about trying to save things, as if we could go back to a better time. By the time we started to think about a future where things wouldn't be saved, our work started to become a memorial - we were becoming scribes of a disappearing world, recording things for posterity.

It's funny how your perception of your life's work changes, depending on who you're doing it for. I have spent more time leading this rag-tag little kingdom of rural humans than I was a research scientist, and many view me as Mother, Chief, Wisdom-Keeper, though to me it seems that most don't listen to the real wisdom I hold. More than anything, they needed a savior, and that's what I became. They are all so young now, and happy because they don't know what they could have had. And I am old, and happy for them, all things considered. But mostly I am alone because few know what it was like and, when I die, the things I know firsthand will become legends.

I'm not sure where the story starts, so I will tell you about one place it began. My parents were a little different: not exactly Luddites, but they did not go in for things like phones and the internet. They always told me they were tools, but not masters, and they didn't want me to grow up like a zombie, face in my devices all the time. My God, keeping friends was hard in school, because back then, that's how you kept up with people. I begged and pleaded, so they let me have one eventually, with all sorts of rules for its use. I remember the day that Mom came into my room with the air of ceremony one would expect for a talk about sex, and gave me my first Communicator. She wouldn't let me get an implant, but she allowed me a Wearable. She was happy for me, but somewhat sad and resigned. My mother told me that they didn't want to make me a pariah, socially isolated, but I think they feared that they had lost the battle against society's vices.

After all of my begging and cajoling, I saw something in my mother that made the Communicator not matter so much. It may seem silly now, but it was the first moment I remember feeling like an adult. I saw that my mother put aside something that mattered to her, even if she felt it was right - because she cared for me. Of course, she had spent her whole life caring for me, enduring much greater suffering than that. I had even appreciated her and loved her. But in that moment, I understood sacrifice, and it was the moment my brain and soul tasted what it was like to be an adult. I agreed to the rules and limits she set with utmost sincerity. The fact that I was not an adult yet eventually led me to break those rules many times, proving my parents right, but I accepted the consequences and turned out to be a much better student, listener, and thinker than many of my zombified pals. I could've been better without the damn thing, but then again, I had my fun, so I can't regret it too much.

When I was twenty-four, I tried to marry a boy named Theodore. He was sexually gifted and terribly romantic, and I will not apologize, even now, for being a total fool for him - to do so would only perpetuate the idea that one should always be sensible and practical in matters of love, and that's not a world I ever wanted to live in. (I never wanted to live in the world I occupy now, but that's an entirely different matter.) My grandfather used to sing an old song, saying, "I don't care what they say, I won't stay in a world without love," and I strongly felt that living a scientific life should not overshadow the unquantifiable aspects of love and romance.

Theodore, however, was not a good choice for a lifetime, and I was happy not to marry him in the end. It turns out that the love that saved me was that of my parents and friends, who waited with me in my princess wedding dress as the minutes of his absence ticked by. Yes, I had a princess wedding dress, the flowers, the tablecloths, the hair with jewels and flowers tucked in. Does that surprise you? I was a very romantic girl back then!

Anyway, Theodore was beautiful and sensitive and passionate, prone to great highs and lows, and perhaps not as eager as I was to make a permanent alliance. I seemed to ground him and thought I was rather a good catch, as I could tolerate his moods, even admire them, without getting too upset myself. I had my own work and was self-sufficient emotionally and intellectually, so that when my work or his separated us, I was happy enough on my own. I didn't pine for him, but was also happy to fall in love all over again after a separation of a few weeks. I knew his every unspoken signal, the change in the wind of his emotions. So when he still hadn't arrived a half hour prior to the wedding, most people wouldn't have worried - anyone could have gotten stuck in traffic, or taken too long getting ready; other grooms could have spilled coffee on their shirt, or misplaced the ring. But I knew Theodore, and I knew he had changed his mind. "Mom," I said, and as I sat down, I gently removed the beautiful veil I had chosen, with butterflies woven into the lace, and placed it in my lap. All eyes turned to me in astonishment, and my mother asked them to leave the room and fetch my Dad.

Looking back on this now, it seems like nothing at all, but back then, when we had our ways of doing things, our communities, careers, status - it was quite a big deal. But once it happened, my heart was relieved and I knew I would survive the embarrassment and rejection. I found that a jilted bride actually gets quite a lot of sympathy, and Dad simply made an announcement while Mom and my girlfriends took me back home and to bed. When Theo called me a week later, he expected wrath, but received none. That emboldened him to hope for reconciliation, but just as I knew him, he knew me. All I said was, "You're one of my butterflies," and he understood. In my grad work, I had devoted myself to cultivating some endangered species of butterfly, raising them so that they would be safe from parasites and predation, to increase their numbers and the genetic diversity of their species. Letting them go meant that they would be at risk, but they weren't meant to be kept. I always knew it was the right thing to let them free. Theo wasn't meant to be grounded, and I wasn't meant to be his keeper. I never spoke to him again.

When I was thirty, one of the butterflies I had cultivated went extinct in the wild. My grief was unbearable. I set off to hike the Appalachian Trail for six months, to immerse myself in nature and to get away from the knowledge that gnawed at me: that perhaps it was all too late.

When I was thirty-four, the bee numbers hit a crisis point, and by the time I was forty, the angiosperms had begun to fail - the bees and other pollinators had been so reduced in number that there weren't enough around to help them reproduce. One by one, crops, then industries, began to fail, and after that followed economies and political systems. Grandpa used to have a droll saying: "Sometimes in life you're the windshield, and sometimes you're the bug." I started to wonder if my lifetime would be one in which I would be a witness, or a victim, of civilization failing. I never thought it would be my destiny, but I wondered about people who lived at the end of the Roman Empire, or who lost their lives in concentration camps in World War II. They probably never expected their lives to go that way, either.

I remember that I was out on a field research assignment, about three weeks in. I was in a high meadow, inventorying whether some native plants had declined in the absence of a particular beetle. Though it seemed that my work had become more of a requiem than anything else these past few years, I reveled in the sunshine and the sweet smell of the grasses in the wind. It took me half the day to realize that something was different: the distant buzz of delivery drones that sometimes flew through the valley below had ceased. And then I noticed that I had not heard any planes overhead. I looked up and saw no contrails, no glint of sun shining off a silvery fuselage in the distance. I remembered my mother telling me about being a young girl on 9/11, having been sent home from school, and the strange, sad days that followed. She said she had never thought much about the flight path over her town, taking for granted the constant and invisible presence of jets whining across the sky, gleaming in the day and blinking their lights at night - until they weren't there anymore. That week that the FAA grounded all flights was unprecedented, and in a world turned upside down with horror, the absence of the airlines was held by more than one person as an unnerving symbol of a changed world - like the silence of a kitchen at midnight when a clock that has always been there stops ticking.

That day in the meadow, I was hardly out in the true wilderness - I had a cabin and there was a town down in the valley. I had my A/R connector for work, but in those days, going into the field was a respite from the bad news, and I kept the connection off most of the time, using it just to log my data. All those years after I had begged my parents to get connected, I had wholeheartedly adopted their ethos. Staying plugged in, especially with an implant, you would get the news whether you wanted it or not, and all you would hear was about the riots, or the apple farmers marching; there was the beginnings of a pandemic in Asia that had shut down intercontinental travel. The blight in the Smokies was being attributed to a die-off of detritivores five years previously. Without these decomposers, plant matter was piling up on the forest floor, simultaneously depriving the forest of nutrients while spreading the blight instead of breaking it down. Rory Musk, son of the famed inventor, had unveiled a plan to send out millions of nano-drones as pollinators to save the crops, but I knew that it was impossible, and unsustainable - even millions was nothing compared to the biomass of the insects Earth had lost. Before entire species started dying off, there were 10 quintillion insects at any given time. Quintillion! And that didn't even include other invertebrates, which matters to an entomologist, and should matter to you. If I've told you anything of worth, please make sure to pass this on: worms, spiders, and millipedes are not, and never were, insects!

In any case, these are the things that make me quiet sometimes, even now. I am sorry. And back then, I could not bear to hear them all the time, so before I went off on that last field assignment, I checked in with my mother and father, and confirmed our meet-up place in eastern Pennsylvania should disaster strike, as we had taken to doing in recent years. I didn't connect the A/R device until I noticed the drones and planes, and by then, it wouldn't connect anymore.

I wish I could tell you the history of what happened, so you'd know, but all these long years we only have our own experiences to piece it together. We know there was a pandemic from all of the quarantines, which kept us out of the populated areas, and kept us from finding each other for a long time. Even out in the wilds, the smell of death came to me on the wind for a month, at least. I'm sure there were natural and man-made disasters as well - abandoned structures, even whole cities, leaking their vital fluids, causing fires... maybe there were wars, if there was anyone left to fight them, but I couldn't know.

Afterwards, it's not as if we lived like cave people - if only it were that simple, living off the land like our ancestors. We still had our knowledge, some of our technologies, and modern resources that we adapted as best we could. I used a manual truck for as long as possible, siphoning gas where I found it, as the self-driving and electric cars were all off-line. I stayed out of any settlements, even though there was no one to man the sawhorses that read "Stop: Quarantine Area" on the road into towns. In a way, that was far more frightening than the first time I had gone down the mountain. I had made my way to the first town, but was stopped before I reached the checkpoint by National Guard pointing machine guns at the truck, barking, "Turn around!" I tried the empty interstate, but the first three exits had concrete barriers across them. Terrified, I turned around on the median and headed back, not knowing when I could next find gas, and decided to head back to the cabin, where I holed up for a few weeks.

There, the solitude I usually cherished almost drove me mad - the world had fallen apart, and I didn't know anything about those I loved, whether I would survive, or anything at all. I knew I had to try again.

My destination was the meet-up point I had decided on with Mom and Dad. I packed up some gear and all of my food. This time, I tried the opposite direction of the town, and came to an abandoned service station. Remember, this was a more rural area, so most of the people were still using manual gas cars. The power was off, and there was no way to work the pumps, but there were several cars parked for repairs, I guess, so I siphoned enough to fill my tank and put the rest into some old-fashioned gas canisters that I found in the shop, and was on my way.

I had never really thought about it before, but the activities of people invisibly maintained civilization. It had only been about three weeks, but without cars driving on them, or road crews to maintain them, the local roads had a thin covering of debris on them already. I recalled a few thunderstorms in recent weeks, and the evidence had not been worn away by constant traffic. A few miles down the interstate, a tree had fallen across the right lane. I saw a snake sunning itself in the middle of the warm pavement, and a minor rockslide had redirected a small stream to run across the highway. And everywhere, leaves and sticks from the last storm had pasted themselves sporadically along the highway.

Yet all was passable, and I eagerly ate the miles away, each exit barred and eerily quiet. I looked for signs of life in the houses along the way, finding none. And then, ahead, even though I couldn't believe there were no people, I also could not believe that I was seeing one. It was the tiny figure of a little girl, pulling a wagon, with a dog by her side. She had turned as soon as she heard me, and stood staring. It was the first time I met your mama, Chelsea.

She doesn't even remember this, and so I've carried the regret my whole life - but when I first saw her, I was afraid. I stopped a hundred feet shy of her, and she started towards me. I opened the door and called for her to stop, trying to be forceful, but not frightening. She did, and must have told her (very obedient!) dog to sit, as he did so even though his tail would not stop wagging. Dear old Charlie... he must have been older in dog years than I am now, but had the heart of a pup. Chelsea and Charlie were peas and carrots. I like to imagine that Charlie was her parents' baby before she came along. Maybe they called him her "brother;" maybe they were a happy family...

I did not want to become infected, and I wanted to get to my parents, but I also could not leave this child. I remember thinking that she must be frightened; I remember softening my voice, and gently calling to her, "I don't think we can come near each other just yet, but I want to help you." She nodded her head, looking serious, and I called out questions and instructions to her, which she did her best to answer. I told her to be brave while I set out a plan. I set up my tent at the side of the road and kitted it out with blankets and food. I told her that she and Charlie could live in the tent and I would live in the truck and, after a few days, we could get together. Then I withdrew the truck about fifty yards back on the road.

It seemed like a sensible plan, but even as I tell you now, I am so ashamed. I could see her and keep an eye on her, but she was so small and so alone. For the first few hours she kept calling to me, statements and questions that grew increasingly heartbreaking. As darkness came on, she called out, "Lucy, I'm scared. Can I just come be with you?"

And finally, I said, "Yes."

***

With Chelsea and Charlie in tow, eventually we came to a bigger town with two or three exits, where you could see the town and several houses off of it. That's where we found Kyle and Evelyn, but mind, they weren't "Kyle and Evelyn" yet - they were just the last two refugees from the town, and after everyone else was dead and quiet, they had each made their way to Route 80, hoping to flag down anyone who was left. They wouldn't have had much in common beforehand, including that Evelyn was twelve years older than Kyle, and looked even older, having had a couple of kids in her late teens that were already grown and gone. But you know as well as any that they became one of the happiest pairs we've ever seen.

We used to read books about downfalls and post-apocalyptic life, and people in those stories were always suspicious of new people and tended to get all "Lord of the Flies." The one good thing I discovered in my second life was that when we found Others, we were so happy, so relieved. It would have surprised me before, but once it actually happened, it seemed like there was never any other possible way to behave except like when a pet dog sees another pet dog and they run over, bouncing, wagging, and sniffing. That happened time and again, which only made me so ashamed of how I had treated Chelsea at first. We mostly found people in pairs or small groups, so if anyone had ever done the same thing with the very first person they found, they never said anything, burying it like me.

Kyle and Evelyn joined our tribe and my mission to find my parents. But over that one hundred mile ride we found just a few more, and I couldn't bring them all, so by the time there were eight of us and a dog, we picked a camping spot at the side of the road and I set off on my own, promising to return in a few days. I don't know why I said that at the time; Chelsea would be looked after, and if I found my parents, I'd be with my people, so to speak. But we were in this together now, so I promised.

I drove around the barriers at Aunt Carol's exit, one of which had already half fallen down, and made my way twenty miles to her house. Uncle Gavin's farm truck blocked the driveway longways, and he had laid a piece of plywood against it. Clever man that he was, he had secured it with a bungee so it wouldn't fall over, and tied a patio umbrella to the truck to protect the sign. I held little details like that to my heart - that at the end of the world, people I loved were still themselves, clever, loving. I wondered at what point he had attached the umbrella. Was it when he was the last one left, knowing that the sign had to last?

The plywood had big spray-painted letters: "STAY AWAY." Underneath, written in marker, were the names of family members and other people they knew. My Aunt Carol's name, followed by "Died" and the date. My cousins, their children - two of whom had died in far off places, reported to them before communications cut off. Delilah, Brian's wife. He must have been the one to tell them, so he was at least alive then, but who knew now? Oh, and the baby...the baby.

Knowing that this was the meeting place for my family, I soon found our names. My mother, and the date she died.

And me. Lucy Caldwell. "Unknown."

Underneath the names: "Love to all Caldwells, Martins, and Nagys. God Bless."

So now I knew. Mom was gone and Dad was brokenhearted, or dead. He wasn't here, and so I thought he probably was dead. But I took a marker and wrote next to my name. "ALIVE! Will return again until I find you, Dad. I love you more than you can know. Stay safe. Food in truck," and dated it. I was running low, but left some canned food in the cab. I felt so selfish keeping my can opener, but I only had the one, so I left a hacksaw blade, and headed back to the rest of the tribe.

After we set up camp on the side of Route 80, and later, right on it because the pavement made a very good foundation for some of our endeavors, I would return to Aunt Carol's from time to time. I thought I would go back forever, but it only took about a year to make it hard to justify. Others in the group had their own ghosts to chase, and I could no longer call it "my truck" or "my gas." And each time I went back, it got harder and harder - trees blocking the road, washouts, and eventually, the fear that I would be stuck out there alone, stranded. The message that I had written was weathered, and I freshened it and added a new date every visit, but no reply ever appeared, and the cans were untouched. I wrote, "If you're alive, head west on Route 80. Love you always." I know if he were, he would have, but sometimes when I get in my quiet moods, I think, "Maybe I should have gone back, just one more time."

***

All we did in those first few months was try to survive, so when I think of my life, it divides into "Before," "Survival," and then, "Anil." I think maybe I would have just gone on Surviving if it hadn't been for him. Our original eight had grown to twelve by the time I had returned from my first trip to Aunt Carol's, and by the time winter set in, we had swelled to twenty-five. We were easy to find, in the middle of the interstate; people joined us in dribs and drabs, sometimes on foot or bike, two on horseback, and a late few who had watched our lights and fires from a distance for weeks, approaching us like feral animals after having been alone for so long - alone and frightened, on the edge of madness. It was two of these who didn't make it later. I think sometimes people survive when it's a matter of purest instinct to find food and shelter, but once those needs are met, the things that are broken inside them are what kills them.

The winter came, and with it the trickle of people stopped. If there were any more, perhaps they had gathered in other groups where they found each other and formed their own tribes. In any case, it would be a while until our tribe grew again, and those who had come together formed a family of circumstances. The things that would have separated us Before stopped mattering, and we just built and gathered, and kept each other company. Your Grandpa Anil was one of these, but it took me a little while to notice him - apart from any of the others, I mean.

When your grandfather walked into our camp, I was starting to be a leader and he was just another refugee - he fell on his knees and wept as we ran out to greet him, and like we did with all of them, we took him into our hearts. He was only thirty-three to my forty-two, which would have been out of the question to me Before, when I would have been too vain to be with a man who would see me age before him. But at the time we met none of that was even a question: he was simply a person who had been through hell, and reunited with humans who had also been through hell. All I thought about in those days was organizing supply runs and building things to withstand the winter rains and thunderstorms, and hope this wasn't a year with snow. You have to understand that it snowed more often back then - we'd see it every three or four years in that area, unlike these days, so I was a bit worried about it. I was also busy not noticing that I was now Chelsea's mother. I could call myself a fool, but I wouldn't be so unkind now to someone else who had been through the same.

Anil thrived. He was a people person who saw the value in everyone, making them laugh at the smallest joys, showing interest in their cares. His deep brown eyes fixed themselves on you, listening intently to whatever you had to say as if whatever was important to you was important to him, too, if only because he cared about you. Unlike some of us, he spoke freely about his loved ones - his beloved Opa from Germany, who lived in India and met Anil's grandmother there. Anil hadn't known her but she was the love of his Opa's life. There was Nani and Dadi, his grandparents from Gujarat; his lively parents, twin brothers who finished each other's sentences and apparently married women who were both named Nina; and a radical anarchist of a sister, who was last advocating for coastal refugees in the New Miami camps. He had been able to learn that all of them were dead, except for his sister, Awni. She lived and worked in the camps, and he had not been able to find her so far away. He hoped she had survived, but held no hope of ever knowing. I asked him about it at the time - how he could talk about them so openly, how he lived with not knowing about her. "It's alright," he said. "I know that our love for each other is real, alive or dead. She knows this, too. There is nothing else I can do."

Anil quickly became my right-hand man, ready and able to help me solve a problem or organize logistics. I think because I was one of the older survivors, and because I was the original Savior With The Truck, everyone seemed to look to me. And I looked to Anil as sort of my lieutenant, which he would later mock me for. While he was falling hopelessly in love, I was giving orders and confiding in a buddy. I was too busy for love, except during the night when Chelsea wanted to go to bed. She would not sleep alone, and I didn't know any therapists who could relieve anxieties related to the apocalypse anyway, so every night, she nestled snugly against me, and Charlie laid against her other side, head stretched out on the pillow. I can still remember the soft thump of his tail every time I reached over Chelsea to lay my hand on his silky side.

Throughout that winter, our tribe helped each other, and when we weren't Surviving, we started to tell our stories. Anil listened as I told him of my work, and how most of my career had been a tragedy - a passion that allowed me first-hand knowledge of our impending doom, of watching the web of life pull apart and die, the joy of knowing creatures who had taken millions of years to evolve, and the pain of seeing the last of them. And we started to wonder about the rest of the world and our place in it. Once we were safe, the questions started to come: What had happened to others? Why did we survive? Were we all immune, or were some of us just isolated when it happened? There had to be others in the world, right? The unspoken question was, Is this the end of people? I suppose the others had thought it, but I had answered it in my heart, if not my mind.

Having decided that firmly, it was a devastating blow when Astrid and Marcus told us all their news. We were in the habit of gathering around the campfire in the evenings, and their announcement certainly got everyone's attention. The two of them had been keeping company for some time, and while it seemed a sweet and good thing that they were finding comfort and companionship, I was foolish to not see the next step coming. I just assumed everyone was thinking about things the way I was. Astrid waited for a quiet moment, and then, grabbing

Marcus' hand and shyly glancing at him, announced, "We just wanted to share that we are going to have a baby."

Oh, if I could take back my reaction, allow them to enjoy that moment, I would, I would. What I really did, amongst the shocked but sincere congratulations, was to get up and walk off with one hell of a pissed-off look on my face. I brooded for days, barking orders, and when Astrid tried to approach me after a few of them, I blurted, "What the hell were you thinking?" Thankfully, she just withdrew and, later, never held it against me. Because she is a gentle soul, and thank goodness for that.

It was Anil who broke through in the end. We had discovered a DroneEats warehouse in the industrial section of the town, and were using it as our food source, figuring it was safer (and frankly, less disturbing) than looting a market or homes where people might be dead inside. I was going on a supply run and Anil insisted on coming along. After a days-long black mood, I was getting so tired of being angry and sad, and was glad to have him along. Anil had become my best friend, my salve. I needed company, and I knew it. However, he ruined it quickly by bringing up the baby issue.

"So, want to tell me why you are so mad about this baby?"

I looked at him like he had three heads. Like he had betrayed me. I could not believe how he could ask that - it was so obvious! But that open-hearted man's eyes returned no aggression. It was an honest question.

I ranted. "Look at what humanity has done to the world!" We had blown it, not only for ourselves, but for the other life on it. No other animal had had such a devastating, irreversible impact. All other extinction events in the course of history were natural, not the result of greed and carelessness. Maybe we were a virus that gave the Earth a fever and she killed us off to survive! Perhaps we humans were a mistake and we didn't deserve to continue! But even if we couldn't resist the impulse to replicate ourselves, who would have children in such a world? What would become of them? Was there no end to how selfish we were? Even if they survived, maybe in another two thousand years we'd make a comeback and just finish what we started!

If I tell you I was foaming, that wouldn't be the half of it. But I spewed it out and, spent, finally sat against a rock and cried. He came and sat next to me. After a while, he held my hand, and I let him. My anger subsided, and I wondered what he was thinking. I dozed against the rock, and he closed his eyes and dozed with me. The afternoon passed.

Anil spoke, finally - carefully. "I know that one of your greatest pains is all of the species that will never again exist. Everything that evolved, changed, mutated, survived its way through eons, all of the living things that depended on them, their own unique beauties. They are gone forever."

I nodded; this was a central truth of my life, too terrible, too unbelievably huge to be the legacy witnessed in my short span on this planet.

He continued, "Well, what do you think of everyone you ever loved? Everything that made humans a unique species? Aren't we one more species in danger of extinction?"

It's not that I hadn't thought about that, but there was still the question: were we the one species too dangerous? It's not like I was advocating for genocide, but we didn't have to propagate ourselves, either. Maybe we had our chance, and we should know that we botched it and make a graceful exit. Before I could respond, he gave me another look, and I paused.

"I've been doing the math, and figuring that if we have twenty-five survivors in this small part of the world, there are probably hundreds or thousands of other little colonies in the world. All the people who were on ships when the epidemic hit, the people on islands, out in isolation... Tell me, if you put the last male and female Monarch butterflies in the world in a jar, would they mate and lay eggs?"

"No. They'd need to lay eggs on a milkweed plant. It's the only food the larvae can eat," I said like a pedant, knowing full well what he meant.

Patiently playing my little game, he said, "Ok, how about the last two spiders?"

"What kind?" I said, just to be difficult.

"I don't know. A wolf spider?"

"They'd mate. But then she'd eat the male," I said truculently.

"Forget the wolf spiders. How about two dogs?" I thought of Charlie and if he was ever lonely for other dogs, and if there still *were* other dogs.

"They'd probably mate. But what's your point? Animals do a lot of things humans don't do, and probably aren't a good idea to do."

"Why? Because we have a different idea of being in the world?"

"Exactly. That's what makes us human. We have certain moral codes about things..." I trailed off, realizing I was walking into a trap of my own making.

"So we are more evolved than animals?"

"I didn't say that."

"So animals are better than us?"

"I didn't say that either. I'm just saying we have different ways of looking at things."

"Unique ways of being?"

I couldn't believe I walked into this. But he wasn't being triumphant - he was serious, sincere.

"Look, maybe I am making a point that humans are just another species that doesn't have to go extinct, but what I'm really saying is that doesn't matter. What matters is that there are going to be hundreds of jars around the world, full of the last few people on earth, and you're not going to keep them from laying more eggs, so to speak. It's not even about you, really, except regarding what's going to happen in your own jar. Chelsea will grow up, and if you have your way, she's basically going to be all alone in her old age, with only Alex for company whether she likes him or not." Alex was a twelve year old boy, the only other child in the camp. I hadn't really thought about that.

"Or, you can accept that people are going to be drawn to each other and have babies, and maybe one day we'll travel again between our jars, and we'll mix our genetic pools, and humans will survive. And you can either help and love them when they do, or try to stop them. I know you think you're the boss, but you have quite an ego if you think you can. No offense," he said, looking away nonchalantly.

A few moments passed. I thought. The rightness of his words struggled with the truth of my own, and I still couldn't reconcile the gap.

But then he said, "It's not a question of whether we will survive, or even deserve to. It simply is. The question is, do you want to take part in living?"

That's how my life went from Survival to After Anil.

***

It wasn't long after that that I started to live again. Like all species, we are both fragile and resilient, and if we are not killed off, the business of living requires us to adapt and move on. It had seemed impossible once that any of this had ever happened, that the upward trajectory of human society could ever stop, but when it had all gone, it seemed as ephemeral as tissue paper in the rain. Nations had been built on mere agreements that abstract things like money and authority were real, until it all fell apart and the only things that were real were food and rain, and the person next to you. While it would always be a part of us, it started to seem like that was the dream, and surviving was the reality. But like I said, we were resilient, and we weren't starting from zero as if we were shipwrecked in ragged pants with only coconuts and an inadequate amount of skill at spearfishing. We had access to packaged food, items we could salvage, clothing and fuel and the like. Even though there were still houses in towns, we built our own crude homes - it was just too likely that each house was occupied by corpses. We no longer had interconnected computers, automation, or the systems that ran them, but we could access raw materials and had knowledge to use and create things that we needed. It was a bit like camping, without the ability to go home if you got tired of it.

Stakes were higher when there was no longer an "out," which focused our priorities and what we valued, so that changed us, crystalizing what mattered. I had studied Buddhism and other paths when I was younger, and intellectually understood how the prospect of mortality was supposed to focus you on the present moment, but without any real possibility of death in my Before life, it just never made its way past my mind into my heart. Now, we had people die when they got sick for want of medical technology we simply didn't have, and that changed our perspective. It's really the only way you young ones have ever lived, and I think it has made you happier. You are more present in your lives than my generation was. I think that me and the ones who were left had a great shock and had to go through a lot to become something like how you are naturally. We had to learn to live, and so I married your Grandpa pretty soon after that conversation. Astrid and Marcus had the first Hope, who you never met, but she was a lovely child and we all loved her. And believe it or not, I had only the third baby of the new tribe not long after - me, who had been so against it! I certainly did not name her Hope: once we started having babies, every teary-eyed parent wanted to name every girl child Hope. I even remember "Hoper" being tossed around for a boy once. No, I chose Rosie, because that beautiful little baby brought me such joy, and I wanted her to be named after something beautiful. One of the greatest accomplishments of my life was being able to find a rosebush and give her a real one. She was twenty-seven years old, and still sweet as a child - I showed her how to dry the flower and keep it preserved, and it was her most treasured possession. When she died, we buried it with her.

You didn't know Rosie was my natural-born daughter? No, I guess there aren't many who would remember me actually having a baby; all of the rest of our children came to us. But where I was previously trying to socially engineer our society and make sensible decisions, once Anil came along my perspective changed and we just enjoyed life. We treasured Chelsea and our friends. Music and books came back into the lives of our tribe, and the first spring we all saw together was like the first spring that ever was. We made love all the time, and hoped something would happen, and it did! Well, not at first. I was older and kept losing babies, so it took a while.

When Rosie came along, she arrived with Down syndrome. While it would have been something that had worried me Before, I did not give a rat's ass about it, not one bit. Anil was the one who had the hardest time with it. It really tested his philosophy of letting life happen and not being able to control things, which was what he was all about - what our life was about.

When Rosie was born he could not stop worrying about his baby girl. He worried about her future, about what would become of her as an adult, after we were gone; he worried about the health problems that come along with it - whether she could see, or her heart, about whether she would be taken advantage of in her adulthood, how we would raise her without the developmental resources from Before. My assurances about everything just didn't seem to reach him, and I realized it was my turn to bring him back from the edge, just as he had done for me. Our whole life had been based on that one talk, where he convinced me to choose to live.

I will tell you something that I hope you will hold gently, for your Grandfather's memory, as it was such a vulnerable thing for him. It seems silly now, how everything turned out. But when I finally reached him, I uncovered the real source of his pain. He was being eaten alive by guilt. He cried about whether we had made a mistake, and what a hypocrite he was, ashamed for even thinking such a thing. It made him question who he was.

Not everything has an instant moment of healing. But knowing that I didn't judge him brought us even closer, and every day brought some new joy - Chelsea cheerfully bringing a flower for her baby sister, a first medical crisis come and gone, laying her in the grass and getting happy gurgles when we tickled her tummy with a catkin. Bit by bit, the guilt and pain wore off, until none of us really remembered it. In fact, I hadn't thought of that crisis in years - it was replaced by the life we shared with her. Once she was just a little baby, but she became a big sister to the many that came later. And all of those worries? Well, the only one that ever came true was that she died too young, but she died in her sleep and was never afraid of anything.

***

The first spring, I taught everyone how to pollinate. If the human race was going to survive, we were going to need food. I was astonished at how little my tribe knew about the natural world, even though the news had covered all of the natural disasters that had led to our current state - how climate change had brought about the first Zika pandemic back when I was a girl, to sea level rise wiping out coastal cities, the extinction of so many species and ecosystems, and the crop crises. Even though these had led to our near-extinction, they just did not understand the cause and effect. So I taught them about flowers.

Our first garden was in the median of Route 80. It was a wide, grassy swath, and made a bit of a valley in the center which had managed rain runoff when it was a highway. Now it made a good water source for our little farm, and we planted crops that needed a lot of moisture near the bottom, and hardier ones further out. The tricky part was getting crop seed - the DroneEats warehouse basically had only prepared food and household goods, so it necessitated our first foray into the town proper. I could tell you more about that, but this is a story about flowers. I will tell you that our fears about what we would find in the town were more gory than what we found; I imagine that once the pandemic hit, most people wanted to be home with their families. The businesses had been boarded up as if in preparation for a hurricane, and we avoided the ones with the most aggressive signs, worried that the owners had perhaps installed booby-traps inside to thwart looters, before the end stages made that irrelevant.

Fortunately, the local Feed-and-Seed was one of the not-too-fortified ones, and we were able to peel the plywood off and break the lock. Now, keep in mind, all of the bad stuff had happened in the previous summer, so by that time, they didn't have a stock of garden seed. We really had to dig around in the back room to find some leftover stock that hadn't been sent back, but we did find some. Tomatoes, beans, squash, carrots - all sorts of wonderful things. And tools! The seed was over a year old and some of it did not grow, but it was enough to start. That foray also opened our eyes to more resources, so we kept returning and looting other stores for years to come. We got medicines, clothing, propane, and quite importantly, canning supplies.

Then, I showed everyone how to become a pollinator. I wrote it all down for when I'm gone, because I worry that in a generation or two, they might not remember the hows or the whys, the science behind it. I told them that many plants evolved in conjunction with insects and animals, attracting them with beautiful flowers, scents, and nectar; in exchange, these critters would then carry pollen from flower to flower as they fed, fertilizing the plants so they could produce seeds, and of course, fruit. The fruit worked much the same way: it provided food for animals, who would then disperse the seed in their droppings. Sure, some plants had other methods - corn is pollinated by wind, for example - but so many plants relied on pollinating insects that entire species were dying off, just like the insects that they depended on. Existing trees were still there, but there was a shortage of young trees to take their places in a generation. Many flowering plants, such as the ones we depended on for fruits and vegetables, were having a hard time. So when our farmed plants started to put forth flowers, we spent just as much time delicately transferring pollen between flowers as we did weeding and watering. I taught every person to see the importance of pollination, so that even when we walked out of the village, through fields or woods, or down the town street, we took the time to pollinate trees, flowers, anything that needed it. Our children grew up with it as much as previous generations learned the sounds that animals make.

Today, I continue to teach pollinating to everyone I can, including the travelers that make their way to us, and through our own young ones that have set out on the networks of old roads. Overgrown but established, they carry news and resources much like the trade routes of medieval days. It's a matter of our own survival, but also a way to help the earth thrive again. I know we've lost species - insects, animals, plants - the forests look different today than they did forty years ago. But there have been times when travelers have brought us some plants or seeds that used to grow here, and we help them to grow. I'm always on the lookout for insects, and some that I haven't seen in decades have started to show up again. Even ash trees have made a comeback. And while it gives me hope, it's not the whole story. The land has changed, and other ecosystems have taken the place of older ones. It's hard to say anymore whether one kind of life should displace another. How can you complain about life growing in front of you, except that I remember all of the diversity, all of the beauty, and the balance, and that what I see now is simply the best nature can do, after humans did their worst.

Nowadays I spend a good deal of my time teaching science in the village. I see children who are happy in their ignorance, because they never knew what we had once. I've told them about the Monarch butterflies and the hemlock trees. I've shown them pictures from the books we've acquired over the years, animals they've never known. The children are awed by them as if they were dragons or unicorns, and they might as well be.

I think they sense my sadness as well. Your cousin Mariposa is a devoted pollinator, and I think she will be my next apprentice.

She said to me once, "Grammy, maybe we can bring them all back!"

Inside my heart, I said, "No child, we can't bring back the ones that are gone. They took millions of years to evolve and interact with each other, building interdependent webs. The ones that are gone are gone forever. All that is left is what we have left."

But she is only six, and her eyes are full of hope. So I said, "Perhaps we can, my love. We can try."

I sent her back to her mother's house, watching her skip happily.

And I wept.

Joinery

Jennifer Lyn Parsons

A software engineer by trade, Jennifer is a life-long lover of story with a capital S. Her work has been seen in various magazines and she has published three books, with quite a few more in her back pocket. She counts Jim Jarmusch and Laura Ingalls Wilder as two of her biggest influences. Make of that what you will.

When not writing either code or fiction, she reads books and comics, and sometimes makes things out of wool or paper. She finds joy in making things, be they digital or analog.

The pounding of a mallet against a wood join drowned out the knocking on the door for quite some time. It wasn't until her rhythm broke that Regine stopped and listened to be sure it was not her own work causing the ruckus.

"Eh? Come in!" she called out. "Door's always open, ya know!"

It was only the stiff breeze blowing across the fields that made her keep the door shut. Wood dust and shavings would fly around the room, and into Regine's eyes, if she kept it open. A shame, too, on such a beautiful autumn afternoon.

The door opened and a girl of about fourteen slipped in, her rough field-clothes rippling in the breeze.

"Ma'am, there's an old woman here to..." The girl stopped midsentence and changed tack as Regine raised an eyebrow at her. "I mean, there's a traveler here to see you. She just showed up out of nowhere. Hasn't been a transport for days."

"For me? I'm not expecting anyone. Odd, that. She at the guest house?"

The girl nodded.

"Okay, just a second and we'll go over. Unless you need to get back to your father."

"No, ma'am," the girl replied. "It's lunch."

Regine nodded as she took off her apron. The wood dust that was stirred up when the girl opened the door was slow to settle and would be agitated all over again when they left. But that was a mess for later. Right now Regine needed to make herself presentable to whomever it was that had come to the middle of nowhere to see her.

As she tided herself up, she saw the girl looking around the workshop. She didn't touch anything, but Regine saw her reach out as if she wanted to. She noted it wasn't just the finished pieces that the girl was admiring, but the tools as well. After letting her take a good look at everything on the front workbench, Regine raised an eyebrow at the girl, who looked down at her feet sheepishly.

"Come on. Take me to this traveler and let's see what she has to say."

They walked together in silence, but the girl by her side wasn't much of a talker, something Regine appreciated in her companions.

The air still held the last bits of late summer warmth and carried the smell of fresh cut grain on the breeze. A few wisps of white hair escaped the loose binding Regine had trapped it in that morning and she realized she hadn't checked the mirror while she was busy getting the dust off her clothes.

"Elisha, is there dust on my face? Forgot to check the mirror before I left."

The girl looked at Regine's face and shook her head.

"You sure? There's a fair number of wrinkles there. Might've gotten some stuck in the cracks."

With a laugh, Elisha checked again. "Yes, ma'am. No dust. Just wisdom and skill."

Regine harumphed at her, but gave her a wink as she replied. "Cheeky."

The town was large enough to support a market, part of the reason Regine had set up shop there, and with a market came a guest house for the folk that came a longer distance to sell their goods.

It still charmed her that the village was so removed from the rest of the goings on of the Diot that everything about living here was a deliberate act. From the market to the furniture to the food they made, hand tools weren't uncommon and there was a sense of self-reliance at the foundation of the culture here.

Unlike the technology-laden central planets, there was only a transport a couple times a month. Beyond that and some of the bot-driven harvesters, there was little in the way of automation here. Having left Acking and its excesses behind a long time ago, Regine appreciated the simplicity. Here she could think with a clear head; fewer people meant it was easier to control her gifts. No more pounding headaches and confusion about who was talking to her and who just had a busy, distracted mind.

When they entered the guest house Regine's eyes took a moment to adjust. When they did, she found herself staring at an ancient-looking woman sitting by herself in the common area. Despite her apparent age, the woman sat erect, her posture straight and eyes bright as they approached.

"Aye, there ye be," the woman addressed Regine. "This young

one 'ere was quite a help in finding ye. Saved these old bones some searching, she did."

Before Regine could reply, the woman stood smoothly and gestured to her. "Come now, we gots work to do you and me. Grim work it is, too. Best be getting on with it."

"I'm sorry," Regine held a hand up. "Do we know each other? Have we met? What are you talking about?"

The ancient woman sized Regine up, then turned to Elisha. "Thank ye for yer help. Best be getting back to your da now. 'E's got more work with yer mum being in the family way, yes."

Looking very confused and a little upset, Elisha replied, "Uhm. Yes, ma'am, but...my mum's not having a baby. She's... she's been gone eight cycles now. The plague took her."

"Ah," the old woman frowned. "I gets the dates wrong from time to time, me. Must've been you in her belly I was seeing. You just go along then."

Elisha nodded, a wary look on her face as she left the two older women on their own.

When the girl was gone, Regine turned to the woman. "Okay, I've got work of my own to do so what is this all about? Who are you?"

"Best we walk and talk, m'dear. Back ta the workshop. You'll be needing yer tools."

With that, the woman headed for the door, turned north, and started walking towards Regine's place without missing a beat. Throwing her hands in the air, Regine followed her, struggling to catch up. The woman moved fast for one who appeared so frail.

Once she caught up, Regine grabbed the woman by the arm,

intent on stopping her. A shock ran up her arm and her eyes filled with a vision of her own life, jumping from moment to moment. Her youth, then middle age, followed by a moment from childhood. Thalia appeared, at first looking as she did the last time they were together, a colorless vision of loss. Then they were young again, falling in love, the memory brilliantly saturated in color. Other memories took form, her parents, that fancy party on Acking with a well-to-do young man, her gifts manifesting, deciding to leave with Thalia no longer there to hold her in place.

When she let go of the woman's arm, she could not tell how long it had been since she grabbed it in the first place.

Out of breath, as if she had been running, Regine paused in the middle of the street and stared at the woman, who smiled gently back.

"Ah, dearie, tha's naught to be messin' about with. But ye've learned yer lesson 'aven't ye?"

"Who...who are you?"

The woman shrugged. "Some folk call me fancy names, legend and such, but ye can jes call me Grannie Hella."

Regine gave her a confused look, but Grannie Hella didn't offer any more explanation, turning instead to continue down the road. Now more curious than frustrated by her interaction with the older woman, Regine allowed her to lead the way back to the workshop.

As they walked, Regine kept an eye on Grannie. There was something about her that felt, for lack of a better description, doubled. It had been decades since Regine had used the skills the Hanturri had taught her, but she did her best now to remember them. A few slow, deep breaths later and Regine had a few clearer words for what she felt around the older woman. It was as if Grannie was two people at the same time, though the second person felt like they were next to her, rather than within her. It was baffling, but it did not feel dangerous, only sad.

* * *

The sun was bright, the afternoon warming as the breeze of the morning slowed enough so that when they arrived Regine was able to leave the door open to air out the bit of stuffiness that had accumulated while she was gone. Grannie Hella took a quick glance around as soon as she crossed the threshold.

"For now, ye'll be makin' a box. Do it up in some kind of wood that smells nice and won't rot easy."

"Could have just said you wanted a commission. No need to come all the way out here for me to take your order."

"Ah, I'll be waitin' fer ye ta finish it this afternoon, see. Then we'll take it and a good sturdy shovel outside of town."

"Outside of town? Where? What are you talking about?"

"I'll know the spot when I sees it. And as fer what I'm talkin' about. I'll tell ye a bit more when the box is done."

"Why should I do this? Why'd you come to me, of all people? Plenty of better woodworkers out there."

"Ah, good smart questions. Yer not like some I meet, all youth an' bluster wit their 'eads in the clouds."

Grannie paused, placing a gentle hand on the bag still slung over her shoulder.

"Tha gift ye've got, tha's wut brought me to ye. Tha special piece of ye whats let you see folks' thoughts? Aye, I know ye gots it. No use tryin' to cover it up wit me, lass."

Regine sat down hard on a nearby work stool. "I... no one knows about that except... did the Hanturri send you? I've kept a low profile, just like we agreed."

With a gentle smile, Grannie shook her head. "Twernt them dogmatic fools wut brought me here. No. They'll have a reckoning, but that's a long way off now. Either way, I've naught to do wit them and they wit me."

"But my gift brought you here? How? Why?"

With a twinkle in her eye, Grannie asked, "Worth the price of a small, sturdy box ta know the answer?"

Taking mental stock of her current work, Regine glanced around the room. There were a few orders in progress on the workbenches around the shop, but the most urgent one was in a gluing rig and work couldn't continue on it for at least two days. Everything else was ahead of schedule and, after all, it had been some time since Regine had the chance to work on something small and quick and fine.

Even more than that, there remained the question of that second presence, and Regine was truly curious what that was about.

"Alright," she replied. "I think it'd be worth it. What size does it need to be?"

***

Sawdust floated through the air as Regine ripped boards down to size, soon followed by the satisfying scrape of a planer bringing them into true. The sweet smell of cedar filled the air as she worked.

It took a little while nowadays for her hands to warm up and her joints to relax in the work. She did not know how many more years she would be able to run the shop, working on her own as she did, though she was reluctant to give up her independence and the quiet solitude she had found here. However, the deep purple bruise on her hip from dropping a heavy board last week was a harsh reminder of her age, and though the wood she worked now was smaller and lighter, she was more careful than she had once been.

Grannie Hella's request was simple: a plain box, hinged, with a sturdy latch. Without allowing the rest of the design to run away with her, Regine made perfect, pretty dovetail joins to hold the box together that also fulfilled Grannie's request that it be self-contained and not need any glue. There was no carving or edge decoration to be done and the final box was elegantly simple.

As Regine worked, Grannie made tea and knitted on some small project she pulled from a pocket. She also hummed to herself, occasionally rambling quietly under her breath, but nothing she said made any sense to Regine. It was all nonsense and seemed to be about events long past and, possibly, events yet to come. Yet oddly enough, Regine could sense nothing of her thoughts. Grannie's mind was the quietest she had ever been around.

There were rumors when Regine still lived on Acking. Running with a dangerous crowd there meant you knew folks from the lower levels of Torant City, and it was only her gifts manifesting that had saved her from a dark and dangerous fate. Before she had to go to the Hanturri for help controlling her gifts, she knew people who frequented the black market underground and they brought back tales of an old woman whose electricity never went out like everyone else's. She and the house, and the alley cats she fed, were all neat and tidy amidst the grimy deterioration, and it was said that she had lived there for centuries.

Of course Regine had blown the stories off as fantasy. Even with the Hanturri's seemingly miraculous powers, the idea of someone living for centuries was the stuff of legend. Now though, with Grannie Hella here in her own workshop and having felt the strange and ancient power flowing through her, Regine began to take those old rumors to heart.

***

When the box was complete, Regine lay it on the workbench where Grannie Hella had placed her bag and knitting. The ancient woman—though having spent an afternoon in her presence Regine now doubted she was actually human—picked it up and examined it carefully.

"Aye, this is fine, fine work. T'will do nicely, I thank ye," she said with a gracious nod.

"I've held up my end of the bargain, fair and square..." Regine began, but Grannie held up a hand to silence her.

"An ye'll be wantin' to know why I came 'ere and to ye."

Nodding, Regine took a seat on the opposite side of the workbench, her legs tired and hands aching. Fine work like that made her realize her hands weren't what they used to be.

Grannie pulled her bag closer and undid the large buckle holding it closed. As she did so, Regine could feel the air shifting in the room, as if there was a storm coming and the pressure had just dropped.

As Grannie pulled a bundle out of the bag, she spoke gently to it, her voice sad.

"'Tis alright now. Ye're almost at rest. Jes a wee bit longer. If ye have the strength, ye can surface for a wee bit. 'Tis safe here."

A moment later Regine heard the sound of someone waking from slumber echo through her mind. The presence of a young woman expanded outward from the bundle and Regine could almost see her standing next to Grannie Hella now, posture straight, a woman of power and grace. She also noticed Grannie was watching her reaction.

"Aye. 'Tis the Bright One ye'll be seeing now. Lovely girl, bit of a fool."

"Grannie, I was no such thing. I could not have abandoned my destiny any more than you could have changed it."

The voice now in Regine's mind was clear and commanding, though she could not place the accent. Grannie sighed at her words.

"True, true, girl."

"Who was she?" Regine asked Grannie, and then realizing that, unlikely as it was, the young woman could hear her, corrected herself. "Who are you?"

"The daughter of a long line of women who are bound to that sword," she replied, pointing at the bundle.

Grannie pulled back the covering on it, revealing the brilliant-white hilt of a sword. It gleamed and glowed almost as if it generated its own light. However, around it was wrapped a disembodied hand, cut off at the forearm, old blood dried into the cloth that enclosed it. Regine sat a bit further back on her stool at the sight.

"It's mine, you know, that hand," the young woman explained as Grannie covered it up again. "I fought a horrible, destructive man and defeated him, but it cost me my life."

"Aye, lass. It did," Grannie smiled sadly. "The Ilandu are defeated fer now. Can't say I'm pleased wit the cost, m'self. But wut's done is done."

"For now?" the Bright One turned toward Grannie, an intense look upon her face. "Do not tell me they will return. What was all this for? I died so my daughter will not be tied so to my own fate. I broke the curse."

"Ye did, and ye didn't, m'dear." Sitting up a bit straighter, Grannie placed the bundle back into the bag and picked up her knitting again. "There's more to come, but 'tis not yer burden now."

"You knew." The young woman balled her hands into fists. "You knew and you did not warn me. This truly was all for naught then. What will happen to my daughter? Is she to be the next sacrifice? If not her, my granddaughter yet to come?"

Making a calming motion with her hand, Grannie did not meet her anger. "T'werent for naught and ye know it, girl. Ye bought a century of peace for the galaxy, at the least, and tha's no small thing."

"But my daughter, Grannie. And her daughter after, and the one after that. What will happen to them?"

"They'll be heroes, t'same as you." Grannie shrugged and picked at a stitch that had not set cleanly.

The Bright One sighed, her shoulders slumping. "Yes. I know they will. Just as my mother was and hers before her."

"Aye," Grannie replied with a matter-of-fact tone, though Regine noted the look on her face betrayed a deeper sadness and resignation. "'Tis what it 'tis, m'dear. Naught we can do 'about it. Though 'tisn't all bad, is it?"

The young woman smiled. "Indeed. There is good in all this as well."

A moment later, Grannie cocked her head to the side, as if she were a dog listening for some far-off sound. "We best be on our way. There's work yet to do."

She turned her attention back to Regine. "We may be needin' ta sleep out overnight. Ye've got supplies fer tha?"

"I...overnight? I might. Got an old tent. We'd need to bring a cart to tow it all. Don't think I'm hale enough to carry a pack anymore." She paused, realizing what she was saying. "How far are we going?"

Grannie shrugged, a look on her face that appeared she was making a wild guess and had no real idea. "Depends how long it takes ta find tha place wot feels right."

"Feels right?" Regine asked. "Feels right for what?"

"To put the Bright One at rest," Grannie replied, and there was such sincere sadness in her voice that Regine stopped asking questions and rose to gather what they would need for the trip.

The weather report looked good for the next day or so. No rain forecasted and the temperature wasn't due to get too low either. Regine was able to quickly rig up the little cart she used to collect downed branches into something serviceable for carrying their supplies.

She climbed up into the attic to retrieve the tent, pleased to find it intact. Along with that, she found a box containing a small camping cookset and fire-burning stove. Thalia had bought them for her as a birthday gift when they were still struggling and Regine realized the memory made her smile now, rather than cry.

***

The cart was soon loaded up for an overnight trip, including three days of food and water because Thalia would have Regine's head otherwise, were she here. The woman was always over-prepared for everything, even to the end.

The cart had handles, but also a harness so it could be pulled along while the hands were kept free. Grannie offered to take the first shift after gently tucking the bag containing the sword bundle in safely. After Regine had asked three times if she was sure, Grannie grabbed the harness from her hands and marched off, heading farther from town. Regine smiled and shook her head, following behind.

Despite the work she had already done that day, Regine found she was enjoying the walk. Early autumn was just right for this kind of journey. The travelers were neither too hot nor too cold and the smells of the fields and stands of trees were deeper and drier than they were in the spring. The land was preparing for slumber at the end of a cycle of life. Regine knew how it felt, though she didn't feel quite ready to lay down all her burdens just yet.

They walked mostly in silence, but for Grannie occasionally murmuring to the sword bundle and the quiet whisper Regine heard in her mind. The Bright One was still with them, though Regine could feel her fading quickly.

Dusk came upon them as they reached a wooded area no farmer

had claimed as their own. It was a sheltered, quiet place to make camp. Between Grannie and Regine, the tent went up quickly. Dinner was simple and warm and they made a bright little fire to pass the time until bed.

The Bright One had been quiet for the last few hours and Regine wondered if she would see the young woman's face again or if she had gone too deep into whatever rest she found in her limbo state. Yet while they sat watching the flames, Grannie pulled the bundle out from the cart and placed it gently near the fire.

"One las' time, my girl. 'Tis soon time fer rest, but ye've got ta stay wit us fer now."

Once again Regine could hear the sound of someone waking. It wasn't like stretching or yawning, just someone coming awake after a peaceful slumber. All in one moment there was a wakeful presence that had been sleeping before.

When she spoke, the woman's voice was strained. "Grannie. I cannot hold on much longer. I must be released or I will be trapped."

"Ach, dear. I know. But ye've got strength in ye beyond wot ye know. Ye can hang on a wee bit longer. On the morrow, ye'll be free to join wit Tir once again."

Feeling that she may be intruding by listening to the conversation, Regine made herself busy stoking the fire. As she walked around it to avoid a fresh billow of smoke from a too-damp log that smoldered, she came to Grannie's other side and the bundle that held the sword and the Bright One's severed hand. There was a palpable energy around it that drew her in, like a child with outstretched hands begging to be picked up.

"Can I... Can I see the bundle for a moment?" she asked, the two women turning their attention toward her as if they had forgotten she was there.

Squinting at her as if probing for some elusive answer, Grannie nodded. "Ye may, but be gentle there. All must stay as it 'tis."

With a nod, Regine put her hands out to gently lift the bundle of cloth.

It still surprised her at times, to see the wrinkles on her hands. The battered nails were no shock, carrying the scars of her work was a badge of honor. The signs of age didn't truly bother her. Thalia often teased her about her lack of vanity, to the point of farce, she would say. It was more that the passage of time came as a surprise, though the number of shelves and dressers and baby cradles she had built in the last twenty years should have served as a solid enough reminder.

Gently lifting the bundle, Regine was surprised at how light it was in her hands. The sword hilt had to weigh less than it should have for its size. As she held it, she tried to open her mind to follow the paths of connection the Hanturri had taught her to see, though it had been so long since that time, she wondered if those doors were still open to her.

A faint image appeared in her mind's eye of a woman who looked very similar to the visage standing before her. She wielded a sword in her hand, the same as the one wrapped in the bundle in Regine's hands. That image was soon replaced by another, then another, the connection going back further and further, each image a woman looking similar to the one before her, each holding the same sword.

Eventually losing count, the images continued for some time until at last there was an explosion of white light before her eyes and their cozy little camp came back into focus. Grannie was giving her a hard stare.

"Ye saw the genesis then. The place where tha sword came to be here in the All That Is."

Regine nodded and placed the bundle back down. "So many women. Mothers and daughters, on and on..."

She looked up at the visage, still present, watching her.

"What is it like, to be part of such a legacy?"

Hard eyes met her own. "To know that my lineage is tied to a fate not of our choosing? It is a burden."

Nodding, Regine looked down at the bundle. "I have no lineage of my own... no one to take the mantle after me. I'll leave nothing behind. I often wondered..."

The Bright One's hardness softened. "I...it is not a curse, to tell the truth, simply a burden. I am sorry if you feel you have given nothing to the world, but I am sure that is not true. Grannie would not have trusted you otherwise."

Looking up, Regine focused on Grannie Hella. Something about the ancient woman's calm demeanor rankled her. "Well? What have I brought the world? A few bookshelves?"

Grannie remained implacable and shrugged. "'Tis not only what ye make with yer hands that gives ye value to the world."

She met Regine's eyes and the woodworker felt suddenly overwhelmed, her emotions rattled and confused. She shook her head.

"I wasn't a mother. Never wanted to be. I loved an amazing

woman, came here and learned my trade. When I'm gone, all that'll be left is the work of my hands."

Grannie shrugged, unshaken by Regine's terse reply. "There be one at least who'd carry on when yer gone, if ye'd let 'er in."

Elisha. The girl eyed her tools every time she came in the shop. She often visited and seemed to make up reasons to stop by, running errands for folks she had no cause to meet with in her regular tasks. Something about her reminded Regine of Thalia and so she had kept her at arms length.

"Perhaps," Regine admitted.

With a pat on the woodworker's arm, Grannie stood and turned toward the tent. "Think on it, m'dear. Plenty o' time. Plenty o' time."

Regine's sleep was fitful that night and she woke unsure what she had dreamt or how many dreams she had other than knowing Thalia had been in every one.

Grannie was already up tending to the cart, and Regine made quick work of heating the little wood stove to warm their breakfast before they headed out.

Still unsure of where they might be going, the morning was spent wandering the edge of the wooded area. It was past Midday and after a brief stop for lunch when Grannie pointed across an open field.

"Tha's the spot. Ha. Knew I'd remember it when I saw it."

A craggly, old tree stood at the center of the fallow field long ago abandoned by a farmer. As they approached, Regine once more felt a pulsing energy, this time coming from the tree.

"Ah, 'tis a good protector, this one. T'will make a fine spot fer the Bright One to lay down at last."

The mood of their little group shifted unexpectedly. As Grannie pulled the bundle out of its bag, Regine felt her throat tighten. Following the ancient woman's lead, she retrieved the box she had made just the day before from the cart as well. Had it only been a day since she met these women? They had become like family to her so quickly and quietly she hadn't noted it until now.

Grannie lay the bundle on the ground next to the tree and Regine lay the box down alongside it. Next, they retrieved the shovels from the cart and, with Grannie indicating the correct spot, they began to dig. The ground was soft and it did not take long to have a hole waist deep.

After cleaning themselves up from their work, Grannie and Regine knelt side by side before the box and bundle.

"Right, child. Time fer ye to rest a' last."

Grannie gave the bundle a tender stroke before placing it in the box. Feeling a tear break free from her eye, Regine was overcome with a sadness she had not felt for many years. She had seen this young woman's lineage and knew things of the galaxy's darkest corners that she could not unknow. The loss of the Bright One became her loss as well and when they began to bury the box she had to pause repeatedly to wipe away the tears that blurred her vision.

When the task was done, they quietly packed the tools back onto the little cart and headed back towards home. Their progress was slowed by Grannie stopping occasionally to make notes on a map, though the few glimpses Regine caught of it looked nothing like any map she had ever seen before. It was full of winding paths they did not take and landmarks that did not exist.

Their conversation started up again, slowly, the further they walked.

"Ye've got tha thinkin' face on m'dear. Me, I knows tha look a wee bit too well."

Regine nodded. "Just considering a few possibilities."

"Aye." Grannie grinned, the first smile she'd cracked all day. "Would it be yer legacy ye'd be thinkin' about now?"

With a nod, Regine realized that, without her noticing it, she had decided to offer an apprenticeship to Elisha.

"Of all the strange things to happen in this odd journey, that was the last thing I was expecting, if you ask me."

The decision brought a lightness to Regine's heart. They talked more as they walked, about motherhood and choices and children of the heart.

Each time they paused for Grannie to mark her odd little map, Regine would ponder what she was going to say to Elisha and wondered if the girl truly wanted to learn from her or if there was simply some novelty to the tools in her workshop. That thought made her a little nervous.

Dusk was coming on when the workshop came into sight. Her stomach did a little flip flop when Regine saw Elisha dressed in rough work clothes, sitting on the wooden bench outside with a book in her hand. Taking a deep breath to settle her excitement, Regine chastised herself for acting like a feather-headed girl and tried to remember that she was an elder and a respected member of the community.

"Not home with your father then?" she asked Elisha as they approached.

The girl shook her head, looking a little nervous. "Harvest is done and he said I could do as I pleased. Is it alright that I sit here? This is my favorite bench."

"What do you like about it?" the woodworker asked her.

Placing the open book face-down on her lap, Elisha thought for a moment. "It's well made. Solid. The wood doesn't fade in the sun. I like the dips that don't hurt my tailbone."

Regine chuckled. "Anything you'd change?"

Elisha sat up straighter before answering. She seemed unsure what was going on, but answered with clarity.

"I would put a low little back on it, just enough to give some support."

With a nod, Regine turned to Grannie. "What do you think, Grannie Hella?"

The ancient woman patted her arm, though this time the contact did not come with any visions.

"M'dear, ye know me thoughts on things. Ye just go wit yer gut and it'll be jes fine."

Regine nodded and turned back to Elisha. "Alright. Inside with you and we'll chat about a few things after I see Grannie here off."

The girl stood and gave them both a little half bow before going inside and shutting the door behind her.

"She's a good 'un. Ye've made a fine choice there." Grannie

smiled at Regine as she grabbed her bag off the cart. "I'll be off, me. Don't think we'll be seeing each other agin for a bit, so ye take care now."

Regine nodded, a sad smile on her face. "Thank you, for...for everything the last few days. Come by again if you can."

Grannie nodded and gave her another pat on the arm before heading down the road toward the village center. When she turned a corner out of sight, Regine headed into her workshop, setting her shoulders as she opened the door.

"So," she said, letting her voice boom with confidence. "Let's talk about the tools you're gonna need to make those changes to the bench."

Crone, Chronos

Cathrin Hagey

Cathrin Hagey is a writer, blogger, and editor based in the Canadian prairies. Among her favorite things: family, dogs, primal grasslands, the Canadian Shield, containers, plant-human hybrids, San Francisco, and a LOTR collectible plaque signed by Virginia Lee. Her work has appeared in New Fairy Tales, Luna Station Quarterly, Kind of a Hurricane Press, Huffington Post, and elsewhere.

I saw it after Jerry gave Mom a black eye. I had to get out, coward that I was, and I let the screen door bang behind me, knowing it would make him even madder. I crossed the street and followed the ravine, that treed-up scar in the land with a foul creek at the bottom, thick with scum. Then something caught my otherwise scattered attention: a house in the weedy lot where none had been for at least ten years. I stopped. Jerry's words from the day before came back. He had been talking to Mom, trying to drive a wedge between us, as if he could. He said, "Your kid's weird. She likes girls." He was right on both counts. I'm a lesbian—and weird, but only because I declared my undying love for the best friend I've ever had and now she won't return my texts or even look in my direction, not even in Mr. Selznick's calculus class when she needs my help.

The house had a cottagey feel to it—scalloped trim along the eaves, moss-green front door, brown bricks smothered in ivy. I normally would have been more curious about its sudden appearance, but my stomach had been flipped inside out from trying to imagine my life without Angel Perez.

I was about to turn around, pass through a stand of trembling aspen to plunge down the ravine for a smoke, when—*squee*—the door opened halfway. There was nothing to do but watch as a bread-loaf of a woman appeared, dressed from neck to ankles in a purple gown, and something else which was wrapped around her head, more tourniquet than kerchief. She peered in my direction, opened the door wider, waved. She looked like an apple doll come to life.

I stared, until she called: "Lilianna!"

Of course I wondered how she knew my name, but at the same time, she looked familiar enough to make me toss off caution like an ill-fitted cape. I crossed the street, then the front garden. The woman's face at this distance was more golden brown crepe paper than dried apple. Her eyes were black, like mine, but the skin around them had a folded pastry quality. Grey fuzz peeked out from the kerchief to frame her face. The lines in her forehead were the furrows of a field. Her lips framed a generous, joy-filled smile.

As I mounted the steps, she said, "I wasn't sure you would come. But I made mint chip ice cream, just in case."

I couldn't help blurting, "That's my favorite."

"I know."

I split in two the moment I crossed the threshold. One part of me was thinking: Idiot—you just entered the home of a stranger because she offered you something sweet to eat. The other part felt completely at ease, as though I'd returned home, finally, at the end of an epic quest.

I followed the woman through a narrow passage lit only by natural light through the front door, which I had failed to close. The farther we went, the dimmer it became, until her purple gown was as dark as a fresh bruise. Relief finally came when the hall opened up to a tidy kitchen with large windows overlooking an

English-style country garden where hollyhocks loomed over ox-eye daisies, and lilies of various hues grew scattered about.

The woman said, "Please have a rest." She pointed to a small wooden table across from the window where two low chairs sat ready. I took a seat and continued to watch the flowers, drinking up their aliveness as though their violets and crimsons, yellows and pinks, could paint over my gray mood.

She removed a glass jar from the freezer, turned, smiled. "Ready for ice cream?"

I nodded.

"You haven't said anything about the clock," she said as she unscrewed the lid. "I thought you would have noticed as soon as you came in."

I followed her gaze to the wall opposite the window. It was painted a bright shade of blue. Mounted there was what appeared to be a sculptural tangle of iron lines and curves. Toward the center the various bits and pieces wound downward, like the swirl of water as it runs through a bathtub drain. Though the overall effect was of motion, the entire thing seemed frozen in time.

"I don't understand."

She bobbed her head and winked at me. "You will...one day." Then she turned around, rolled up her purple sleeve to reveal a surprisingly well-muscled forearm, and got to work scooping ice cream.

I stood up to take a closer look at the clock.

"Don't touch."

"What if I do?" I turned around in time to see her lick the spoon with the glee of a child. Then very slowly she set it down and began to clap her hands. As my expression grew more puzzled, she clapped faster, her smile widening to reveal a row of teeth crowded in a familiar pattern. My heart skipped a beat.

"In case you don't know, I'm applauding your inquisitiveness. May you never stop asking 'What if—?'"

I slumped back into the chair, keeping my eyes on the strange wall hanging. For an instant its threads seemed to squirm and dive like so many worms undermining earth. When I blinked it stood still.

"Is this one of those numberless clocks no one can read? My mom put one in our living room. But I don't see any hands. How does it tell time?"

She put the jar back in the freezer and carried two bowls of ice cream to the table. "I call it a clock, but in fact it's a motion-time converter. You wouldn't be able to comprehend the logistics of the thing—not yet, but the heuristics...I think you're already on the way to understanding, if I've got the timing of this visit right." Her black eyes gleamed.

Before I could ask her to explain what the heck she was talking about, I heard: "Lili." The voice was distant. The croak of a crow.

"Did someone call my name?"

"Stay here. I'll be back in a few minutes."

I spooned ice cream into my mouth as she passed me. It was so cool and sweet, for a moment I considered doing as she asked. But as soon as she passed the window and began her ascent up a short flight of stairs, I got up quietly, leaning against the wall for support as I peeked up after her.

She went up slowly, as though each step took a toll. When she got to the top and turned left, I followed, tiptoeing the way I did at home when I was trying not to disturb Mom and Jerry.

The stairway was narrow and each step was a wood slab worn smooth from use, depressed in the middle. The walls were also wooden, buffed by time. At the top, I peered around the corner as she entered a room. I made my way there, soundlessly, and then stood just outside the door, pressing my ear against the wall.

"Is she here?"

"You aren't supposed to know about that."

"Of course I know. I'm not dead yet."

I wanted to see the second speaker, so I risked getting closer. My fingers found the edge of the doorframe, and I held myself up while leaning to one side, seeing part of the way into a cluttered bedroom. A small chest of drawers was heaped with books, shawls, knitting needles, balls of yarn. I could see the end of a bed and a threadbare blue and white quilt. I heard the old woman say, "It's all right, Angie. Don't get riled up."

My heart beat like the wings of a startled bird.

Then the older, deeper voice: "I want to see her."

Without considering that the old woman had asked me to stay behind for a reason, I went in. The smell of lotions and putrefying flesh hit me hard.

"No...no," said the old woman. "You weren't supposed to follow."

She sat on a low stool beside the bed, her purple gown flowing over her scrunched up legs. An ancient figure lay in the bed—a thin-shouldered, wispy-haired, prune-faced, glorious being.

"Lili," she croaked, and I went to her, bending to be nearer, as if it was the most natural thing in the world—to kiss the ancient being on her forehead.

"Angie," I said. My mind was shocked to see my love in such a state, but my heart seemed to understand so much more.

Then I turned to the old woman in purple. Our black eyes met. The pain in her hip seared my parallel joint.

"You are me."

She nodded.

"But Angie and I are the same age. What happened?"

"Time doesn't tick at the same rate for everyone. Angel and I lived apart, until a few years ago. Her journey was full of challenges." She nudged me aside and reached forward to pull back the quilt, just enough to reach for Angel's narrow, fragile hand. I put mine on top of theirs. The gesture came as naturally as in a dream. Except this was solid reality.

We remained as we were for as long as it took for my feet to get pins and needles. She seemed to know how I felt, because she put her other hand on top of mine.

"Angie's asleep," she said. "Let's go back downstairs."

I began to cry then, and I knew I could easily lose control, fall to the floor in a sobbing heap.

"Come on. I'll say goodbye for you, for both of us, later."

I followed her back down the stairs. She went so slowly, I had plenty of time to gain control over my feelings. But with each step, I seemed to become heavier and heavier, until, at the bottom, I could barely drag myself back to the table.

"It's one of the effects," she said, taking the other chair.

I took my seat. The ice cream had melted and the spoon had slipped into the bowl. She laughed, the gleam in her eyes returning. "Just do what I do."

We lifted our bowls to our mouths and drank the rich, minty cream. As I did, I turned my stiff neck to glance at the clock. Some of the strands were squirming about as though they'd been kicked.

She set her bowl on the table. "It's nearly time for us to part, Lilianna. Do you understand what's happening?"

I set my bowl down slowly, licked my lips, nodded. "You travelled back in time. I'm not sure why. And I don't know how you—we—did it. But I believe it."

She smiled with pride, as though I were her child and I'd just won a prize. "We invented the clock. The premise is based on the Goulding-Perez hypothesis." Then she picked up her spoon to lick the last of the cream.

"Goulding-Perez?" I said. "But Angie isn't good at math. How did she—"

"She didn't. It was all me. And you, of course." She chuckled. "Goulding-Perez is my married name." She put a crooked, callused finger to her lips. "You know how it works. You will."

I stared into her shining black eyes. They were deep, sharp, kind. I set my leaden forearms on the table. It felt as if the force of gravity had doubled, tripled.

"This is impossible," I said, after a few minutes of silence.

"What is?"

"Time travel. If you really are me, then we've created a loop. It's impossible to time travel and meet up with yourself, because—"

"Yes?"

"The Mother Paradox. You went back in time, met your *self*, and if I don't do all the same things you once did, I won't become you. Since you've disrupted my timeline that's exactly what will happen."

She smiled. "Now you're thinking. But I didn't use a wormhole, dear. I knit myself something far simpler and much more elegant."

She laughed when she saw my expression. But I couldn't help myself.

"I know what you're thinking, Lilianna. That you stumbled into the house of a crazy old lady who talks rubbish and, perhaps, put drugs in your ice cream."

I was unable to move my arms or legs, but my thinking was clear. "What's happening to me? I can hardly hold up my head."

"Want some more mint chip?"

"Don't change the subject."

She got up to clear our dishes. And when the bowls and spoons had been set in the sink, she washed her hands, drying them on the front of her gown. "Ahh, sometimes I'm tempted to be young again." She peered at me over her shoulder. "But then I would have to revisit the bad times along with the good. I don't think I could bear it."

"Do you mind?" I tried to turn in the chair but found I was stuck where I was. "Could you please explain why I can't feel my feet?"

She turned to face me, hands on hips, a posture I recognized. "I thought you would have some idea how the clock works."

I tried to shake my head. It was too heavy.

She came back to the table, scratched her chin. Then she smiled. The creases in her cheeks spread wide.

"I suppose I should explain why I came back to see you, before the clock returns us. It's about Angel."

I wanted to tell her it was always about Angel, but I couldn't move my lips.

"You see," she continued, "she always loved me—you. Us. But I was impatient. I didn't wait for her to tell me. I ran off to Princeton right after graduation. That's why it took years for us to find one another again."

She chuckled when she saw my expression. "You haven't applied to Princeton?"

I slowly shook my head.

"You will."

She took a handkerchief from out of nowhere and dabbed at a tear under my eye.

"If I hadn't been so impulsive, Angie and I would have been together sooner. Her life would have been different. Better. I could have prevented so many things. I've risked everything to come back in time to warn you."

"Yes," I thought. "I will be with Angel. We will be together."

"You wait here. I need to check on her."

Had she forgotten that I had no choice but to wait? Even my breath was no longer in my control. But she floated away as if she were nearly weightless.

Then, after what felt like an hour, they came down the stairs together, side by side, tripping along like girls. Angie wasn't so wizened. Her hair was thicker, smoother, with streaks of black amongst the grey.

"Do you understand what's happening now?" my purple-clad self asked. And when I couldn't respond: "You've already decided to be patient."

I wanted to say: "Now there won't be a time machine. You've changed everything, including my future research." Then I thought, "With no time travel, I wouldn't have been able to return in the first place." It was a classic thought experiment. Nothing special. Yet I'd already seen how limited that thinking was.

Then Angie and I, our beautiful old selves, began to fade away, along with the house and everything in it. I grew even heavier, and was at the point of wondering how much more I could bear, when the house winked out like a candle.

I was butt-to-the-ground in the middle of the empty lot, and able to move again, when my phone vibrated. I pulled it out. Angel Perez had texted: *Need calculus help. ok?*

It was more than okay. But I would play it cool. For as long as it took.

Francie

Leonie Skye

Leonie Skye is a writer and anthropologist. She has short stories in Shimmer and Entropy Magazine, and edits science fiction for small press Elm Books. She lives in Portland, OR with her partner, daughter, and a chihuahua-corgi named Karl Marx. You can also find her on Twitter @leonie_skye or her website: hazylightwraiths. wordpress.com.

She was cradled in the crook of my arm to support her rounded back. We'd left her little motorized chair in the car, and despite its being summer she was dressed in one of her high-necked lace blouses and silver taffeta skirts because she was always cold now.

As the automatic doors yawned open, peach-scented air conditioning swept her knitting out of her stiff fingers and rolled it into the mechanized door tracks where it looked like a dust bunny.

"Oh!" she cried.

I picked it up and patted it back into her lap. "There there, Francie."

I grabbed a tiny herringbone throw from the diaper bag and placed it over her knees, whispering into her fuzzy, gray hair, "We'll just see what we need to do."

As the doors shushed closed behind us, a candy-coated teenage voice called, "Welcome to American Dame!"

Francie looked up from her knitting and smiled tolerantly at the voice, then looked at me and rolled her eyes.

I'd read somewhere that they'd struggled with the name, and you could feel unsaid words lurking in the retail shadows.

Matron wouldn't have worked since American Dame was meant to include childless women, like me. "For women who long to find and nurture that missing piece of themselves," said the marketing. The missing piece was not a child, they claimed, but that's how I'd initially heard it. What else could be meant by a missing piece?

Francie liked to call it American Hag. American Crone. Spinster. Witch.

I stopped to catch my breath and shift the diaper bag higher on my shoulder.

"You all right?" said Francie, brows wrinkling with concern.

"Oh I'm fine," I said, though I was not. "Let's see. Where do we need to go?" I peered up at the graphically slick signage proclaiming aisles for Career, Travel, Hobbies, Feminism, Wardrobe, and Lifetime Achievement.

The candy-coated voice skipped over to us, face squinting with a plump dewiness. "Can I help you?" She reached in and grabbed Francie's hand. "Hi, honey! Oh, what a dear!"

Francie leveled one of her looks at the young woman, gray eyes becoming cold, wet ash. Her soft cheeks sagged into a frown. She put her knitting down with irritated little hands. "We are *not* in need of assistance, young lady."

The young woman giggled. "Oh, you're just darling!" she cried. Then she whispered to me, "Nursing has been moved back behind the yoga center."

"Actually, we're ready..." Here I choked up a little, something I'd hoped I wouldn't do.

Francie caught my eye and gave me her no-bullshit look.

"We're ready for the Passage with Dignity package," I croaked.

"Ah," said the young woman, voice lowered respectfully, hands church-clasped in front of her. "Then you'll want Final Journeys, over near Medical."

Francie nodded sharply and took her knitting back up, pearling two rows with quick rage.

***

"What do you think, honey?" Bob asked with tempered excitement.

The wrapping had just come off and I was still processing what it was I held, so I said nothing at first. That ancient feeling of childhood Christmas mornings competed with dread.

She blinked up at me from out of a box. I plucked out a glossy folded pamphlet nestled at her feet and skimmed through features, ignoring her searching gray eyes.

Shares hobbies, dreams, and advice

Loves bookstores, cafes, and films! Especially science fiction and fantasy!

Preloaded career!

Easy to travel with!

Keeps secrets

Fun to dress up, thousands of accessories for every stage

Sturdy storage and sleeping box may be outfitted with lovely bedding (An asterisk here explained that it was also suitable for her final rest, though a culturally diverse range of cremation packages could be purchased as well.)

"Well, pick her up," Bob urged.

I looked into her eyes and she waved a tiny hand. I placed one palm behind her neck and one beneath her thighs and gently lifted her out.

She was wearing jeans, black Converse, and a nondescript t-shirt, just exactly what I wore most days. She smiled and my heart melted a little. I smiled tentatively back.

"See?" Bob said, grinning.

Our cat leapt off the back of the couch and into my lap, so I lifted her protectively.

Bob laughed. "Oh Dozie, don't be jealous. Mommy has another baby now."

Bob and I had always spent our Christmases the same way. We'd eat breakfast, open a few gifts, take a walk, nap. Then we'd order in Chinese food and watch movies, pausing at some point to have sex. I hadn't been expecting anyone else.

She spent most of that day in a baby-carrier Bob wore to protect her from Dozie. He seemed newly invigorated by her presence, whistling contentedly as he made everyone coffee. She sat facing out, her long legs flopping in their cute Chucks. She smiled at me shyly, complimented the coffee, and tried to start conversations. It was just like what I'd do in similar circumstances, I mused.

But by the time we got around to Chinese food and movies, we were all quite comfortable with each other. She even recommended a few films for our next movie night and was delightfully knowledgeable about the Star Wars franchise. Over fortune cookies, Bob looked at me and said, "Well, whaddya think?"

I knew what he meant. It was time for a name. She knew too, I think, but, like me, wasn't in the habit of inserting herself where she felt she didn't belong, even in the matter of her own naming.

"Well, I think..." I said quietly, eyeing her. She'd taken all of our fortunes and was neatly pinching them together at the edges, trying not to look interested. "I'm going to name her- *you*, I mean... after my Grandma Frances."

She looked up and smiled. "I love it," she said as though she'd put the idea in my head.

***

The teenager retreated amiably to her station beside the door and Francie and I jutted our chins out and plunged into the current of the central aisle, bracing ourselves.

Soft pink and yellow lighting brought out the tableaux vivants to optimal effect. Dames posed as intrepid rock climbers, brilliant surgeons, astronauts. There was even a dame standing, arms crossed authoritatively, behind the desk of a small, perfect replica of the Oval Office.

All of the memories flooded back.

As we passed the Career section with its tiny suits and briefcases, miniature diplomas one could hang on miniature walls, I thought about how pleased I'd been to learn that Francie had come preloaded with her own moderately successful career. She was an acclaimed poet who wrote passionate defenses of the humanities that were widely shared on social media. So I'd started taking her to the American Dame Cafe to read her work, and it was always very well attended.

"I'd love to do what you do," I'd blurted out one time.

"Would you?" she'd responded.

Embarrassed, I'd shown her some of my stories, and from then on she was always my first reader and best fan.

Upon the sale of a first story, she'd commanded me to buy a bottle of champagne. Riding home from the liquor store in her infant car seat, she'd clutched it happily in her arms. And, despite everything else that was going on then, I'd cranked an old punk song and shouted along like a maniac. We'd gotten roaring drunk, and the next day Francie in particular had looked about a decade older.

Now craning to look at the cafe as we passed, that site of so many literary triumphs, she muttered, "Hm. New seats."

I took the opportunity to veer from the aisle and brought us to a table. There were narrow but very tall chairs with ladders, rungs sized to accommodate dolls' hands and feet. I placed her in one and sat down, expectant, hopeful this place might change her mind. She'd reconsider this path. She'd propose a movie instead.

"Look, Francie. You won't have to sit on my lap anymore. Aren't these new chairs great?"

She sat rigid and stared forward, urging me to understand that she was disappointed in me.

I ignored her and looked past the lectern where the space seemed newly elongated, stretching out in a brightening shaft, the far wall dissolving into a sidewalk scene where bodies hurried by busily in a silver rain and dames were silhouetted, drinking citron pressé and coffee.

"A Paris cafe scene? How charming!" I exclaimed. "They've really renovated this place. So high tech."

"If something so fake can be charming," Francie muttered and notched her fingers together. "This wretched place, all these fools pretending at life, using dolls to do the things they can't."

"You don't know that for certain," I said quietly.

"Pick me up please. I'm too tired to make it on my own."

***

The year after Francie came to me, when Bob got so sick and was spending more time in bed, I started drinking heavily and sleeping out in the yard, unable to endure the smell of him, the whistling, labored breathing. His thinning muscles and papery skin.

Perversely, I began stumbling out the back door to the grove of rosemary bushes and lavender I'd once thought would be the ideal place to labor if I had ever become pregnant.

I would stare up at the stars and light pollution and cry myself senseless, letting the police helicopters strafe me with searchlights. I'd wake up in the morning mosquito-bitten and stiff as a dried-out board.

Nevertheless, every morning I went to my job at an insurance company. The anthropology teaching jobs had all dried up and the only work I could find was creating protocols and lists of Best Human Practices so that the company could rate their customers' lives on risk scales.

I'd come home from this every day feeling like a giant old pencil eraser had rubbed out all but my outlines.

One night, as I lay in the yard, Francie came pushing and marching through the herbs. She crawled up onto my chest and slapped me hard across the mouth. "Pull it together!" she whisper-screamed. Shocked, I sat up and she stood back, tiny fists on her hips.

"Oh Francie," I wailed, "he's all I have!"

"Wrong," she'd seethed. "You're all he has. You have me. This is why I'm here."

"What? What do you mean?"

But she simply took my hand in her petite little raccoon claws, and I began to feel the fury getting grounded, dissipating.

And that was the first time I noticed how she could take my terror into her own body and sink it there like toxic sludge in sand.

Francie would let me do her hair. It was the same auburn with threads of gray as mine. I'd French braid it, or put it in pigtails with brightly-colored plastic bands I bought at the drugstore.

I watched it change, getting grayer and wiry, light as wisps of shredded fiberglass.

I made her clothes and built her a small house in the backyard were she liked to read and write. Bob, who was then in remission, did the carpentry. To my very fussy specifications, he made her a desk that looked out on the herbs so she could watch giant praying mantises, green iridescent beetles, and leaves that were, to her, the size of beach umbrellas.

"We have to get this just right, Bob. Writing is her passion," I told him.

Sometimes I'd sit on the patio and just watch her working, writing in her journal, typing feverishly, reading with her feet up on her desk. I'd bring her tea and bourbon. I urgently wanted for her to have everything she needed for her art.

***

Bouncy, inspiring music wafted through the retail space like yet-to-be-spooled cotton candy. Francie hummed minutely along with it, looking perkier than she had in the cafe and seeming to have forgiven me.

As we walked past the Wardrobe department, the memory of our first big fight crashed into my head.

One day I'd noticed she had retired her Chucks and begun wearing sensible shoes. I managed not to comment, though it pained me. But when, shortly thereafter, she began selecting high, laced collars and long skirts in the Seniors aisle of the Wardrobe department, I pitched a fit.

"Is this really what you want to wear?" I snickered.

"Yes," she said, glaring at me. "Why?"

"A little Victorian, don't you think?"

Nearby customers glanced over at our raised voices. Other women clutched their dames who were sporting stylish pant suits, printed scarves, heels, and even mini-skirts. I was furious. "This is not what I had in mind," I hissed violently.

"Even the people closest to us can surprise us sometimes," she said. "Imagine if you had to deal with a teenager!"

"I'd prefer that!" I shouted. "This is so fucking old. I thought you liked fashion."

At this point, we'd done some traveling together. We'd bought each other Spanish boots and Swedish clogs. We'd purchased matching violet Hello Kitty backpacks in Harajuku. But none of these things had come out of her dresser in a very long time.

"This is what I like now. People change. I'm not particularly fond of my décolletage, for your information. And I quite like lace. My body, my choice. If you want to get a mohawk and a tattoo, go right ahead. Live your own life."

Bob died not long after that fight. The cancer came ripping back with a vengeance. This time, I stayed in bed, stroking his forehead like I always imagined I'd do with the child we'd never had.

We were able to afford in-home hospice because he had a very high Best Human Practices rating, even with the cancer, so when they transformed our bedroom into a hospital room, I pretended the blinking lights were the dashboard of our spaceship.

I marveled at my ability—as though standing outside myself—to let a person die next to me. I thought distantly, So this is what it's like. This is what it is to hold the hand of your best friend as the life and heat leaks out of them.

In my anticipation of the event, I imagined I would rip the bed up, take a hammer to it, a lighted match. I'd howl at the moon. But I did none of these things.

After the funeral and a small gathering, as Francie and I sat before the fire in the vast emptiness of what had once been a cozy, modest living room, pans of half-eaten, grey-tasting casseroles scattered about, I asked her, "What did you mean that time?"

"What?"

"About... this is why you're here?"

She ignored this question and asked me one instead, as was her way. "Why did you name me after your Grandma Frances?"

Swallowing down irritation, I answered. "Oh, I don't know. Maybe because she was the one who gave me dolls. Every year for birthday and Christmas. And I guess... I always thought if I had a daughter I'd name her Frances."

"Hmmm," Francie mused.

"Now how about answering my question."

"You're an anthropologist, don't you know? Some dolls are meant for times like these."

I took another sip of camomile tea and watched the fire's breath play Francie's wispy, silver hair. I said, "What, that... dolls are miniature versions of ourselves? Humans develop through play? All that?"

"That and... other things too."

I looked at her. "What do you mean?" I was being intentionally obtuse, I knew. I hadn't yet admitted it to myself, but the truth of what Francie was, what I'd made of her, was dividing cells inside me and beginning to make itself known. But I wanted her to say it.

"A doll is a twin, a double, someone to attract and absorb evil that may have otherwise come your way during dangerous times. And maybe also hold on to things and ideas for you so they don't get lost."

She slid off the couch and went to stoke the fire. "And sure, we try things out for you, help you imagine yourself differently."

But Francie was not like the dolls I'd played with as a girl. The main point of them always seemed their appearance, whether I was dressing them in glamorous gowns and punching little diamond studs into their ears or, in later years, shaving their heads and swapping their body parts. They were cheap physical propositions, theories to be tested.

With Francie, what I wished to see play out was an ideal internal life. I'd sit in a low deck chair on the patio, sipping wine and watching her literary life in the miniature house bloom and unfold without anxiety or interruption. I took pride in it and would stop to arrange a lock of her hair, or scrub a smudge off her cheek.

When Francie had first come to me, we seemed the same age. Soon, though, I couldn't pretend that she was not accelerating along her trajectory, first years and then decades ahead of me. Everything about her was fast. She was prolific with her work, no nonsense in decision-making. She was up before the dawn and late to bed at night. She learned everything without effort.

Soon, I watched her enter peri-menopause. "No big deal. Icy drinks, popsicles," she told me. "Lots of exercise. Sex. Erotica. Yoga. Organic food. You've just gotta keep everything limber and well-oiled."

It is hard to express how much relief these demonstrations brought me. Everything that would eventually happen to me would have a labeled shelf, a set of numbered boxes in which to catalogue them and lay them to rest. For, I could see now that I was passing through the same stages as Francie, just a few long paces behind and well-buffered. Idly, I wondered if I would eventually develop Victorian sartorial tastes.

When her hot flashes finally faded, she seemed to settle into an especially regal version of herself. She took to wearing her hair in a poofy but neat bun and reading glasses around her neck.

Everything seemed fine.

But one evening, I came home from work and couldn't find her. I went out to see if she was in her office. But it too was empty, the little desk lamp off. I called her name.

I went to the clearing in the herbs and found her lying on her back, staring up at the sky, blinking, dissected buds of lavender strewn over her silver gray skirt. Her hair fanned out around her head, white amid the red and orange leaves.

"Why didn't you answer me, Francie?" I asked, annoyed.

"Who's Francie?"

Fear knifed through me. I came down slowly and sat beside her. "You," I said. "What do you mean?"

"Oh," she said as the confusion that had fogged her face moments before evaporated. "Sorry, I'm just so tired."

We went into the house and, as we started dinner, she told me about how full-up she was, how her body was turning to glass and paper, becoming inert. She'd taken all she could for me.

"It shouldn't be long now," she said.

I was enraged. I burned myself, almost intentionally, on the pasta water. I sputtered out meaningless, unfinished sentences. "Who will I have now? After you're gone, what do I have? A horrendous job and this stupid old body!" Finally, I shouted, "Dolls aren't supposed to die!"

"All we ever have is our own stupid bodies," she'd said very calmly. "But jobs can be gotten rid of. Now help me finish this sauce."

***

We passed the yoga center and observed women and their dames all engaged in downward facing dog. I envied them. They would finish their practice and then go have a light dinner and see a movie.

"The next Star Wars is just a few months out, you know," I said, failing to keep desperation from my voice. "You could stick around until then, couldn't you?"

Francie said nothing, as though she hadn't heard, as though my voice was just part of the insipid soundtrack now.

Arriving at the counter, we could see over in Nursing the convalescing dames in their little beds or seated in comfy chairs next to windows with leafy green views. Some played checkers or bridge.

A young woman appeared. "How can I help you?"

I froze, speechless, so Francie took over. "Our time is at hand," she announced, which I thought was rather an ominous way of putting it.

The young employee looked at us, expecting further explanation, so I said, "We're interested in the Passage with Dignity package."

"Oh, I see," the young woman whispered and nodded swiftly. She turned to open a cabinet. I watched all her movements with dread, thinking them too fast. She pulled out a little envelope and placed it on the counter. "Okay, let me just..." and she took Francie out of my arms.

A tear rolled down my cheek. From the young woman's arms, Francie stared at me, through me.

The woman lifted Francie's poof of gray hair and touched the back of her neck. "Oh!" she exclaimed. "I'm not sure... Did you purchase this doll here? Or, perhaps from a knock-off dealer? Or..." The woman blushed.

"Um, why?" I asked and Francie continued to stare at me, her eyes looking suddenly black.

"Well, there's no..." She lowered her voice even further. "There's no serial number." She turned Francie around quite gently so I could see.

"Is there supposed to be? My husband bought her."

"Yes, see," she said. "Right here at the base of the neck, there should be a number."

I stared at her and picked Francie up again, frankly relieved to have her back in my arms, though she felt stiff. The woman took up the packet from the counter and placed it back in the cabinet. "I'm afraid we can't administer end-of-life services to a doll that's not one of our own. I'm sorry."

Out in the parking lot, Francie mumbled, irritated. "Ridiculous. I'm just exactly the same specs. Fit all their clothes, accessories. Everything. Ridiculous."

I didn't speak all the way home. I didn't know what to say. When we pulled into the driveway, Francie said, "We have everything we need. It's simple. And you have that syringe still, yes? From Bob?"

"What are you talking about?" My hands shook on the steering wheel.

"I need you to help me die, that's what I'm talking about. The worst is over now. It's safe to take things head-on. Take some responsibility. Release me."

I watched her get down and shuffle into the house, still mumbling to herself.

I sat in the car for a long time staring at the facade of our house and there was a quality to it I'd never seen before, almost like an old photograph of someone I'd once known well but who'd moved on and probably forgotten me. It was a house located somewhere in the past. Take responsibility, I heard it say.

All at once I recalled a note that had come with one of my childhood dolls, written in my grandmother's hand. It is natural to give these dolls your rage and the pain of growing up, it said. Let them take some of the immediacy. But they'll rot with it and will need to be destroyed in time. Be merciful, it concluded.

When I finally came inside, Francie was up on her stool, rummaging through food in the pantry, dragging pots onto the stovetop with her voluminous skirts all tied up like old-fashioned riding bloomers. She'd been out in the yard already. There were piles of sticks, herbs, a neat stack of leaves, a tumble of dead green beetles.

"Francie..."

She flipped through a small black book I'd never seen.

"Francie!"

"What, dear?" She turned and glared at me over her reading glasses.

"I can't... Please don't... I'm so sorry. You're so much more to me than that."

"Oh, it'll be fine, love," she said, smiling warmly. "It's just that I've been ready for some time. And you're ready."

***

So there I was on a summer evening, out in the back yard in front of a fire pit, holding a tiny, elderly version of myself in my arms and weeping.

Francie had cooked the serum and loaded it into the syringe. She'd said, "We'll wait for the new moon. That'll give us a couple more days together and then, poof! And it'll be harder for neighbors to see the smoke. Anyway, they'll just think you're burning yard trash."

But we didn't need the syringe after all. She declined rapidly in our last days. She sat in my lap and let me braid her hair as she watched large bugs ambling by or the sudden showers of water drops off leaves.

She began insisting she was not Francie. She was Bob's cancer and my failed career, she said. She was my daughter, of course, the one that would never ever be. She said she was a collection of expectations and theories never put into action. She was debilitating anxiety and disappointment.

She was all the dark and dangerous thoughts that had hurled or inched toward me during our time together. She was Bob's cessation of breathing and my skipped heartbeat. She was the creeping through the house with a lighted match, the impulse to scald with the teapot, the pills in the medicine cabinet.

She said she was out of her mind now, floating above herself somewhere. She was a cabinet of small drawers in which to put all these facts, which could be taken out later and considered dispassionately. She was a version of me.

Then she grew quiet, curled up one last time, and died.

In the pause that ensued, I braided her hair tightly as though to secure it against storms, high winds. I washed her brittle body with warm, lavender-scented water, dressed her in her favorite silver skirt and blouse, her little sensible shoes. I wrapped her in her herringbone throw. Then I placed her light, fragile body atop the fire. It was gentle, not roaring.

The smoke carried us up into the black, starry sky.

After a little while, in the hushed night, I began to hear the tink, tink tink of small hard things falling like hail on leaves and stalks of grass, on the roof of her little house.

I got up and walked through the yard, collecting shards and placing them in my pockets as I went.

Cry Sanctuary

Anna Catalano

Anna Catalano is an honors graduate
of the University of Oregon, where
she earned a BA in English. After
graduation, she interned at Tremr, an
independent blogging site, creating
content in the form of witty and
analytical film reviews. Recently,
Anna returned from DISQUIET,
an intensive two-week creative
writing workshop in Lisbon, where
her work was critiqued and shared
amongst international authors and
publishers.

Twenty steps from the bedroom to the kitchen.

Fifteen, if she moved quickly enough, but it wasn't worth the risk.

Josiah was sleeping heavily by the time that Tuppy had gathered
the will to inch herself out of bed, stepping carefully around the
old creaky floorboards in the middle of the room. Her favorite
cotton sweater lay balled up on the floor in front of the closet,
and she kept both eyes on the bed as she stooped to pick it up.

Empty bottles littered the hallway, tossed haphazardly as Josiah
had stormed off to bed the night before. Tuppy hesitated in
the doorway, listening to the cadence of Josiah's breaths as she
waited for her eyes to adjust to the dark.

It took close to three minutes to cross the length of the hall. She
stared down at her stockinged feet until they toed the edge of the living room carpet. The jigsaw puzzle on her craft table beside Josiah's
La-Z-Boy chair lay in pieces, as it had for several months now.

Tuppy's chest tightened. It would never be finished now.

She knelt in front of the kitchen sink, cursing the cracking of her
joints. Thankfully, the cabinet hinges didn't creak as she eased
it open. Behind the pipes was the box of swiffer dusters, and

Tuppy fished through the soft rags to the modest roll of dollar bills that she'd stuffed at the bottom.

The bed springs squeaked from the bedroom.

Tuppy froze.

What reason could she give for being up and about at eleven at night, kneeling on the kitchen floor? She'd thought she'd heard a racoon? Possible, but they hadn't had a pest incident in weeks. Her cheek burned and twitched, and she dug her fingernails into her palms.

A minute passed. Then two.

It wasn't until she was certain that she hadn't heard a single footstep that Tuppy very carefully let out a breath through her mouth.

A sudden heat crept over her skin as she got to her feet, sweat beginning to bead at her neck. Her bottle of Paxil sat in the medicine cabinet in the bathroom, but it would surely rattle— and Tuppy would have to creep past Josiah's personal study to get there.

The thought sent cold shivers through her overheated body.

Ten more steps to her slip-on shoes at the front door. She pulled on her sweater, slipped her feet into her shoes, and shoved the wadded up cash down her shirt.

And stared at the doorknob.

He'd hear the click for sure—Tuppy eyed the living room window and considered whether it would be any quieter to crawl out into the bushes.

The early onset arthritis in her right hip loudly dissuaded her.

The second hand of the grandfather clock ticked louder and louder in Tuppy's ears the longer she stood, sweaty fingers slipping against the lock. *Just get outside,* she repeated to herself. *Just get outside and the hard part will be over.*

She clicked the lock, turning the doorknob as far as it would go before pulling open the door.

The brisk night air rolled over her like a balm, but Tuppy's muscles remained coiled even as she stepped onto the porch and closed the door behind her.

Three blocks to the bus stop. And after that—

After... that...

Her legs were stiff as lead by the time she reached the stop, the city noises dissolving into static around her. She eased down onto the bench, which was abandoned save for an old sandwich wrapper with part of a sandwich still in it.

What am I doing? Tuppy's heart clenched in her chest, throbbing in a manner that made her wonder if she would have a heart attack right here on the street corner. *He'll find out I'm gone, he's probably waking up right now, he'll know I've gone to the bus stop—stupid, stupid!—*

As if from outside her body, she watched the approach of the bus, pulling into a smooth stop in front of her bench. Her mind still foggy, her body absolutely frozen, she waved it on.

If I go back now, he won't be too mad, she reasoned, picking at a loose thread on her sweater sleeve. *I-I'll say I was sleepwalking, that it won't happen again...*

She should've taken the gun.

It would've been easy enough to break into the safe in Josiah's study. She knew the combination was 042775—the day before they'd gotten married, nearly forty years ago this month. She had watched tutorials at the local library, sitting in an isolated corner as she took advantage of their unrestricted internet. Certainly it would be simple enough to operate... and she wouldn't be sitting alone and vulnerable at the bus stop, at the mercy of anyone who came along. Or came looking.

But she *couldn't do it.*

She hadn't even noticed that the next bus had come and gone until she checked the ETA board. That had been the last bus of the night. The next one would arrive at 6:30 in the morning.

I have to go back—either that or sleep on this bench and hope, pray, that—

Her throat was closing up, her breaths ragged as she gripped the edge of the bench.

A forest green minivan turned the corner, pulling through the bus lane and rolling to a stop across from her.

The side door flew open and a young woman leaned out. "Hey, are you okay?"

"Oh," Tuppy blinked back at her. "I'm... yes, I'm fine, I—"

The woman glanced down at the hands in Tuppy's lap, her eyes widening at the purpling skin of her wrist.

Tuppy hastened to push her sleeve back down.

"We're like you, you know," the woman said, her gentle voice somehow carrying over the sound of the occasional vehicle passing by. "We all needed somewhere to go. You can come with us."

Tuppy swallowed. "I... I don't know, I—I shouldn't be out here..."

"Please," the woman moved to the side, gesturing inside the van, "before he finds you."

Fear broke out across Tuppy's skin, the image of the .22 flickering in her mind. She had less than a hundred dollars in cash, and it wouldn't last her long.

She could smell his rancid breath on her face, the exact tone of his voice as he snapped—

Tuppy stood, sliding past the woman and into the van.

The door closed and the woman called over her shoulder to the driver. "Take us out, Ethan."

A soft voice from the driver's seat made a noise of approval, and the car launched into motion. Tuppy scrambled for a seatbelt.

"I'm Reina," said the woman, sinking onto the other available seat in the back. She nodded at the driver, whose features Tuppy could barely make out in the rearview mirror. "That's Ethan, and that little troublemaker is Nua."

From where she sat, Tuppy could only make out a tuft of unruly red hair from the driver's seat, as well as a black studded earring in each of Ethan's ears. She couldn't see anyone else in the car, but then a small head poked its way around the passenger seat. The girl looked to be around nine or ten, and she gave Tuppy a shy smile before making several fluid gestures with her hands.

Still tense and flustered, it took Tuppy a moment to realize it was sign language. "Oh—" she turned to Reina. "Is she—"

"Nua's nonverbal, but she's not deaf," Reina explained. "She can hear you."

Tuppy nodded before extending her hand. "It's nice to meet you. My name's Tuppence—Tuppy. Langdon."

Nua shook, her little grip firm.

"How long did you wait?" Reina asked, long strands of her curly dark hair escaping their tie as the wind whistled through the car.

The van lurched as they rounded a corner, and Tuppy grabbed hold of the door handle. Her hand crept inside the pocket of her sweater and found its familiar place around the locket she'd hidden there. "About twenty years," she whispered.

There was a long pause. "...I meant at the bus stop," Reina said quietly. She reached across the seat, her hand hovering just over Tuppy's shoulder. "Shit. I'm so sorry."

"Don't swear in front of the nice old lady!" Ethan chided, weaving the van between the thinning streams of traffic as they exited the highway. "Now she's gonna think we're a bunch of hooligans."

"Dude, the fact that you just used the word *hooligans* kinda makes me think that maybe *you're* the old lady."

Tuppy glanced at Reina's hand, which was still deliberately not touching her shoulder, and nodded. The touch was gentle as Reina squeezed.

"Who are you?" Tuppy asked the van at large. "How did you find me?"

"Like I said, we didn't have anywhere to go. Needed to get out, just like you." Reina removed her hand from Tuppy's shoulder. "We're each other's family now."

"And technically, Nua found you," Ethan volunteered, nudging the girl's arm with his elbow. "Just like she found me."

Tuppy's mind raced, overwhelmed with questions. "What do you mean, she found you? How? What do you all do?" Then, as a delayed reaction: "Isn't she too young to be riding in the front seat?"

Nua turned around to quickly sign something. Reina cracked a grin.

"She said it's okay, her big brother Ethan will protect her. Also, we're almost there."

Tuppy almost asked where they were taking her when she recognized the entrance to Westchester Park on the other side of town. It wasn't accessible to the public, but Ethan turned onto a grassy, overgrown path barely wide enough for the van to pull through.

Once they were deep enough into the park that Tuppy could no longer see the surrounding roads, the van rolled to a stop.

"We can sleep here for the night," Reina announced, looking to Tuppy as she unbuckled. "You can decide in the morning if you want us to drop you somewhere, or if you want to continue with us."

Tuppy stepped out onto the plush grass and stared at the van, parked conspicuously under a black cherry tree. "Shouldn't you, I don't know," she waved at the van, "cover it in branches or something?"

Ethan chuckled as his long body unfolded out of the car, a bundle of lanky limbs. Tuppy had half a mind to tell him to cover up his bright hair, which would surely be a beacon to be noticed amidst the green of the park.

"No one will find us here," he assured her. He opened the trunk and returned with an armful of blankets. "You can have the back of the van, we're more than happy to take the ground tonight."

"Oh no, no I can't have you do that—" Tuppy protested, but Ethan had tossed Reina and Nua two blankets each and they were already spreading out beneath the tree. She watched as Nua curled into a tiny ball, tightening the blanket around her neck and sucking on her thumb.

Reina sat upright, leaning back against the tree trunk. "Honestly, we'd feel way worse about making you sleep on the ground, especially on your first night out."

And Tuppy found herself too exhausted to argue. The kids all seemed comfortable enough on the ground, and her hip felt decidedly grateful for the option of the van. It took some maneuvering to get even the slightest bit comfortable, even on the blankets. Tuppy laid on her back, staring up through the van's skylight at the spattering of stars.

She pulled the locket from her sweater and kissed it, keeping it curled to her chest—warm, pulsing like a second heartbeat—as she willed herself to sleep.

***

When she woke, it was from a dream she couldn't remember, but every muscle in her body was locked, the taste of terror still clogging her throat.

Where am I? She struggled to sit up, momentarily thrown when she didn't hear the creak of bedsprings or smell lingering cigarette smoke. The breaking light of dawn trickled in through clear windows beside her head, and Tuppy exhaled in a rush as she recognized the van. The park was quiet, save for the soft twittering of birds.

Tuppy glanced down at where she still gripped her locket.

Her left hand was gone.

She blinked. Then again, her heart ratcheting up its pace. She felt her fingers curling around the cool metal, but could see only the locket in her lap. Beginning to tremble, Tuppy lifted the locket, watching as it seemed to hover on its own in midair.

Her breath whistled out of her, high-pitched and frantic. "Help," she gasped out, tearing her eyes away to glance at the others still sleeping on the grass. "*Help—*"

Reina was the first to wake, scrambling to her feet when she heard Tuppy hyperventilating. "Hey," she hurried over, eyes wide. "What is it? What's wrong?"

Tuppy could only whimper, holding out what she knew to be her left hand, disappeared at the wrist.

"Wow," Reina breathed. She reached for Tuppy's hand, fumbling for a moment before successfully grasping it. If Tuppy hadn't felt the warmth on her palm, she would've thought that Reina's fingers were wrapping around thin air.

"Breathe, Tuppy, it's alright."

"It's *not* alright," she managed, gripping Reina's hand tighter. "My hand is *gone!*"

"It's not, though, is it." Reina gently shook their joined hands. "It's right here. Now please, breathe. You know your own hand. Remember what it looks like, how it would look holding mine."

Her words made no sense... Tuppy bit her lip, staring at the stump of her wrist. She knew she should see the beige of her skin, the freckle on her pinkie finger, the subtle dotting of age spots that had begun springing up in the last few years—

As she watched, the flesh of her hand faded back into existence.

Reina beamed. "You did it. That's incredible."

Tuppy's hand slipped from Reina's grip and back into her own lap, where she kept poking at it to make sure it was real. "What... what happened? And why aren't you concerned?"

Reina turned to Ethan and Nua, who had stirred from the commotion and were standing several feet away. "Something... happened to all of us, when we left. When we got away from whatever it was we were trying to escape."

Tuppy stared blankly. "What. Do you mean."

Reina thought for a moment. "Ethan, are you okay with keeping watch for a little bit?"

He nodded. "Yeah, I'm good." He waggled his eyebrows at Nua, who giggled, before striding off through the trees.

Reina reached past Tuppy to grab a small Rubik's cube, which must have shifted around in the back of the van. She held it in her palm, looking down at Tuppy. "I don't believe this Rubik's cube exists," she said.

It was a good thing that Tuppy hadn't blinked, because Reina had no sooner spoken when the toy vanished.

She rubbed her hands together to prove that, unlike with Tuppy's hand, it wasn't just invisible—it was completely *gone*.

"So you're a magician," Tuppy said, peering around Reina's body, searching for the secret. Of course, it was an illusion—they must have been traveling performers or something...

But Reina shook her head. "No. I imagined that it stopped existing, and it did."

"So... it's... nowhere?"

"That toy? That exact one? It doesn't *exist* anymore. Now, if I wanted to bring it *back*, I'd have to recreate it exactly—every detail and blemish—and force it back into existence." Reina's eyes closed, her jaw tightening. She jerked her head towards Nua.

The girl was now holding tight to the once-again-existent Rubik's cube, already twisting the blocks at lightning speed.

Tuppy gaped. "You don't expect me to believe that you... that you actually... made that disappear—"

Reina pursed her lips. "Nua, could you give us a minute? Come back when you've solved that."

Nua didn't bother looking up as she walked away.

Reina perched on the edge of the van. "So I was with my girlfriend for three years, right? Kind of a long time to be with someone. For the longest time, I thought we were happy. That everything was fine."

Tuppy waited as Reina paused, her face drawing up and her shoulders going tense.

"She would say things and I'd believe her—things that, in hindsight, I know weren't true. It wasn't until years later, when things got bad, that I learned there was a name for that." She gave a stiff shrug, her lips pulling into a tight, small smile. "The gaslighting made me think the world was one way, when it wasn't. Now, I get to decide what's real and what's not."

Tuppy felt a stab of sympathy as she stared at this young woman, aged far beyond her physical years. "So... now you can make things disappear?"

"And reappear." Reina grinned. "But only if I want them to."

They sat in silence for a while, and Tuppy worked to process everything that Reina had just said and done. She reached for Reina's hand again and squeezed it gently. "I'm sorry she hurt you like she did."

"Others had it worse. Not that it's a competition," Reina amended, "but Ethan... fuck. He was half-dead when we found him. Beaten within an inch of his life."

Tuppy's stomach lurched. "And... the little girl? Nua? She... she wasn't—"

Reina's face darkened. "We haven't asked. And she hasn't told us. All we can do is take care of her—take care of each other." Her eyes fell on Tuppy's wrist, still visible and still colored with finger-shaped bruises. "Want me to make that go away?"

Tuppy ran a thumb over the swollen skin, wincing. The bruise itself didn't hurt much, but the impression of his touch burned hot. "No," she decided, her throat thick, "I need to remind myself why I can't go back."

It looked like Reina would respond, but her attention shifted to the form of Ethan loping back into view.

"I got breakfast!" he announced with a grin, both hands full of fast food bags.

He had no sooner spoken when Nua returned as well, tossing the completed Rubik's cube to Reina.

Ethan handed Nua a bag, then tossed Reina a different colored one. "I didn't know what you'd want, Ms. Tuppy," he said, holding out the remaining two bags and gracing her with a bashful smile. "I just stopped by a few different food trucks and did my best."

Tuppy could already feel the heartburn coming on as she peeked through the contents of the bags, but the boy's face was so earnest that it was worth not having any Pepto. She chose the safest option. "Thank you, dear. I think I'll have this one."

She chewed absently as the sound of Reina and Ethan chatting amongst themselves drifted into the background. She stared back down at her left hand for what felt like the hundredth time. How had that happened? Nothing had felt different or wrong, she'd simply woken up, and it was—

How did I do that?

She'd been dreaming, and bits of memory flickered through her. She'd dreamt of Josiah, but the Josiah of years ago, back when they'd met, fallen in love... before he'd turned into...whatever it was he'd become.

But the dream had shifted, twisted into Josiah's face, warped with rage. His anger, exploding over the smallest thing, his words callous where they used to be tender.

When had he changed? And why hadn't she noticed? Tuppy shuddered, pulling herself back into the present.

With a start, she realized that her fingers were disappearing even as she watched.

She didn't cry out this time—instead, she watched as the invisibility spread, through her hand, past her elbow, farther than it had before—

"Hey, check it out!"

Tuppy looked up to see Ethan lounging on the grass, grinning up at her. He gestured to the now seemingly missing left half of her body. "You're a chameleon, Ms. Tuppy!"

She pressed her arm along the side of the van, just to remind herself that it still existed. It was unnerving, the absence of her body unnatural—and yet, Tuppy felt just as intrigued as she was horrified.

There was a sharp intake of breath, and Tuppy's attention shifted to Nua, who was standing frozen and unblinking, staring into a patch of trees just beyond the van.

"Nua?" Ethan knelt beside her, forehead creased in concern. "What's wrong, sweetie?"

She didn't respond—she barely moved at all.

"She sees something," Reina said, grabbing the blankets off the ground. "We should move."

Tuppy stepped closer to the girl, who was too stiff, her eyes wide and blank. "Is she alright? What's happening?"

"She does this sometimes, she'll be okay," Ethan explained, sweeping Nua into his arms. "It's probably nothing, but we like to keep moving just in case. Shouldn't stay in the same place for too long."

Tuppy accepted Reina's hand in stepping over a mess of tree roots. "What about the van?" she asked, peering over her shoulder and watching as the vehicle disappeared into the distance.

"We can come back for it later. But if there is anyone out there, better to be safe than sorry."

Ethan navigated easily between trees, leading them further into the park, and Tuppy wasn't entirely certain they were still on any kind of man-made path.

Eventually they broke through the thick web of foliage. In the clearing, a marble fountain bubbled at the center of a cobblestone courtyard. Ethan set Nua on the ground at the base of the fountain, leaning her back against the side.

Her eyes were alert this time, darting all around, fingers twitching at her side. Her little body shivered with panic.

Tuppy had seen that expression before.

In a hospital bed in St. Anthony's twenty years ago.

On her own face in the mirror.

"Do you like music, Nua?" Tuppy asked, easing herself onto the ground beside her.

Nua wasn't meeting her gaze, but after a moment, she nodded.

"Would you like me to sing you something?"

Another nod.

Tuppy took a deep breath, and began to sing. The words had never left her, even after so many years. Memories clogged her throat, but she sang anyway.

By the second verse, Nua had calmed, her breathing even. She leaned against Tuppy's arm, which was so unexpected that Tuppy nearly stopped singing.

The song ended, and all was quiet.

"That was lovely," Reina whispered. She and Ethan sat on the other side of Nua, both staring at Tuppy. "What was that?"

"I wrote it years ago—I used to sing that to my daughter when she was your age," Tuppy nudged Nua gently. The locket in her sweater weighed heavy, and she pulled it out, unclasping the latch and holding it open. "This is her. This is Arielle."

The photograph had aged slightly after years of handling, but there she was—her fair hair and emerald green eyes a copy of Tuppy's own. But she had Josiah's crooked smile, back when he would show his teeth for anything but baring them in anger.

Tuppy swallowed, the prick of tears stinging her eyes. "She was twenty-five—about your age," she looked to Reina. "She died giving birth to my grandbaby. I-I never did get to meet him."

"She was beautiful," Ethan said, at the same time that Nua turned towards Tuppy and signed something.

"She said," Reina translated, brushing her own damp eyes, "you would've been a wonderful grandma."

A sob tore out of Tuppy's mouth, and the locket trembled in her hand. "Thank you, sweetheart."

They let her cry for a bit, for which Tuppy was grateful—Nua got to her feet and hopped up onto the perimeter of the fountain. She walked the entire circle before deciding to sit on the edge and dip her feet in the water.

"What happened to her before?" Tuppy asked when the tears had finally dried and her muscles relaxed into exhaustion. "Was it some kind of panic attack?"

Ethan ran a hand through his hair, dislodging bits of shrubbery. "Best way to describe it is astral projection. Nua can leave her body behind sometimes, go somewhere else. It's how she found me, when I was—" he broke off, before shaking his head, the usual dimpled smile returning to his face. "It's incredible, but sometimes it's too much for her."

"She calls it flying," Reina explained. "But I think sometimes she sort of... gets stuck, trying to return to her body."

Tuppy's heart ached. "That's how she found me at the bus stop? By... doing that?"

"I'd say it's a good thing she did," Ethan said, wrapping one arm around Reina's shoulder and holding out his hand to Tuppy, who squeezed it.

***

Nua loved puzzles, which was something that Tuppy felt she should have realized after the girl had solved the Rubik's cube in less than ten minutes. She excitedly described her favorite kinds of puzzle games as Ethan translated, and Tuppy did her best to explain, without a visual reference, how to play chess.

As the sun hung low in the sky, Reina announced that she was going to retrieve the van. "It's been hours, and we should probably move to a different part of town in the morning."

"Can't you make the van appear here instead?" Tuppy asked, half out of curiosity and half hating the idea of any of them splitting up.

Reina chuckled. "It's not just moving things around—to make things reappear, I would've had to make it disappear first. And as much as I hate that butt-ugly van, I haven't zapped it." She shot Ethan a pointed look. "*Yet.*"

"You will do no such thing."

"Besides," Reina continued, addressing Tuppy again, "it's massive and has too much detail. I could probably imagine it gone, but I doubt I'd be able to recreate it properly." She ruffled Nua's hair before walking off. "It'll be fine, Ethan'll take care of you until I get back."

"It's not just that," Ethan whispered after Reina had left and Nua was sitting just out of earshot. "I've asked her... back when things were really bad... if she could—" he waved his hand, meeting Tuppy's eye with grave purpose, "to me. She refused, of course. Said she wouldn't even if she could, because she wasn't sure if she could bring me back."

Tuppy's stomach sank to the ground, a chill washing over her skin. "Oh, Ethan..."

"I haven't thought that way in a while, don't worry," Ethan assured her. "Though it would've been different if I hadn't met Reina and Nua. And you."

Tuppy opened her mouth to mirror the sentiment, but stopped short as the sound of a rumbling engine filled the air.

Ethan stood, cocking his head at the wall of trees that Reina had passed through. "That was quick."

Branches cracked, followed by the groaning of old gears, the sputtering of a backfiring carburetor.

The blood drained from Tuppy's face.

"No," she mouthed, nearly tripping as she stepped backwards until she hit the fountain. "No no no, please—"

"Ms. Tuppy?" Ethan moved to her side, one hand gripping her shoulder. "Hey, what is it? Are you okay?"

"He found me," she whispered, barely able to breathe as Josiah's pick-up truck pulled through into the clearing.

"Nua!" Ethan reached for the girl, who scurried to his side. "Stay behind me, okay?"

The truck coasted to a stop, engine falling silent. The door opened, and his boots hit the ground with a deafening thud.

"Tuppence? That you?" He was enveloped in shadows as the sun nearly finished its descent behind the fountain. The breeze rolled his scent towards her—smoke and sweat and the Old Spice cologne he'd never changed—and Tuppy was back in the living room again, arms wrapped tight around herself as he shattered a vase against the wall.

"Josiah, please," she said, holding out a hand in front of her as if it could bar his approach. "Please, don't—just leave me alone—"

"Leave you alone?" He moved slowly, like a cougar circling its prey, his voice even and deadly. "Like how you left me alone, in our house? In the middle of the night?" He stopped just several feet away from her, shrugging with his hands in his pockets. "What's the big idea, pulling a stunt like that, darlin'?"

Her heart was slamming against her ribs as she forced herself to speak. "I'm warning you, Josiah. Just get back in your truck and go home—"

"You're warning *me*?" Josiah jerked his head back towards the truck. "Listen, I'll tell you what. Just hop on back in the truck, come home, and we'll forget all about this, yeah?" His eyes fell on Ethan, as if noticing him for the first time. "Who the fuck are you?"

Ethan straightened. He was taller than Josiah, though not wider.

But in that moment, he appeared far more formidable than he ever had. "A friend," he said, crossing his arms over his chest. "I'm going to have to ask you to get back in the truck, sir, and leave Ms. Tuppy alone."

Even in the dark, Tuppy saw Josiah's eyes spit fire. "Are you trying to tell me how to talk to my own wife, boy?"

He shifted into a wider stance, and that was what he always did before...

"How did you find me?" Tuppy managed to ask.

He dragged his gaze back to her, letting out a gruff laugh. "You must think I'm a goddamn idiot. You think I don't know that you carry that stupid necklace around with you everywhere?"

Tuppy's fingers tightened around the locket. A cold chill rushed over her. "What—"

Josiah jerked a gnarled finger at her. "They make GPS chips real small now. Bet you didn't know that."

She stared down at the locket, at the face of her daughter. She wondered if she could see the tracking device that had betrayed her. "I didn't know that," she whispered.

"Course not. You've never been the brightest, have you, darlin?" He reached back into his pocket, and the glint of steel in the moonlight sent Tuppy's heart flying to her mouth. "Now I'll tell you again," he said as he leveled the gun at her chest, "get in the fucking truck."

Tuppy was frozen. For all his talk, for all his threats, Josiah had never pulled the gun on her before.

A dark figure caught her eye over Josiah's shoulder, and her eyes flickered up to see Reina, on foot and without the van, standing at the edge of the clearing. The young woman halted the moment she saw Josiah and the gun, then continued sneaking forward.

No, stay away—

Tuppy frantically shook her head at Reina, urging her to stop.

But Josiah caught the movement. He turned to follow Tuppy's gaze—

Movement erupted at Tuppy's side, but she didn't register it, didn't realize that Ethan had rushed towards Josiah as his head had turned—

But Josiah was too quick. He spun back around—

Tuppy heard the gunshot, felt the ringing in her ears, deafening her...

But what she heard above all else was the sound of Ethan falling to the ground, his head cracking against the pavement.

No—!

Somewhere behind her, Tuppy heard a broken noise from Nua, saw her form darting behind the fountain.

Tuppy wanted to scream, felt it building in her, but instead, everything stopped. Static buzzed in her head.

Ethan was crumpled at her feet, and she couldn't look—couldn't breathe—

Her skin prickled, and she lifted her arms in front of her to see that they had both disappeared up to the elbow.

"Josiah." Her voice wobbled, but it came out stronger than she expected. She forced herself to look at him, at the monstrous face of her husband. "*Stop.*"

He turned his glare on her, but his eyes widened as he blinked at the place her arms should be. "What the *fuck*—!"

Now the legs, she thought, imagining them gone. Just like that, they vanished as well.

The gun shook in Josiah's hand and he stumbled backwards. "What the hell is this, Tuppy? What's happening?"

"I know you always preferred me to be seen and not heard," she said as her torso faded into the background, leaving only her head visible. "But now you'll have to deal with neither."

She knew she had completely disappeared when a choked gasp escaped him. He whirled around in a circle, frantically waving the gun as he searched for her.

"Tuppy?! Hey, Tuppence, honey, I don't know what's going on, but you... you don't have to do this, okay? Just—just come back with me."

Tuppy's eyes had already adjusted to the dark, so she knew exactly where the leaves and uneven stones would crunch on the ground. She took a silent step.

Seven steps until she was on the other side of him.

Josiah held his body tense, head jerking back and forth around the clearing.

She kept her breathing shallow, making no sound as she created more distance between them. "You will never hurt me or anyone else again."

He spun, and Tuppy wondered for a second if he would shoot into thin air. But he wiped his brow, his hand shaking more violently now. "Now, Tuppy, you... you know I've always wanted what's best for you, darlin'—just... cut this out, alright? Whatever this is, just stop it—"

Across the way, Nua had bounded from behind the fountain to Reina's side. Tuppy inched closer to Josiah, though every instinct screamed at her to run. To not let him get this close again.

Ten steps until she was behind him, close enough to smell his sweat, close enough to see the mole on the back of his neck.

He whirled around again, and Tuppy made herself a statue, suddenly sure he could sense her. But his eyes were darting from side to side, wide with a fear that Tuppy had never seen before.

He was terrified.

The gun still sat in his right hand, barely a foot away from unknowingly grazing Tuppy's invisible arm. He was flustered, distracted—

She paused, waited for the crushing silence to send him shaking again, and snatched the gun from his hand.

He cried out, tripping on his own feet as he stumbled backward.

It was heavy, too heavy in her hand, and Tuppy's stomach lurched with nausea. It was still warm.

Without waiting another second, she threw it into the trees.

Josiah looked wrecked, his silver hair scraggly and his mouth agape. He fell absolutely motionless, as if bolted to the ground.

Tuppy willed her head to reappear first, strength welling inside her at Josiah's gasp of horror. She met Reina's eye again over his shoulder, and this time, Tuppy dipped her chin into a minute nod.

Reina crept closer, indicating for Nua to stay behind.

"You never really saw me, Josiah," Tuppy said, letting the rest of her body slowly reappear and meeting his stunned gaze. He gaped at her, completely oblivious to Reina coming to a stop just behind his shoulder.

Tuppy took a shaky breath. "I want you to see me, like this, just this once."

He stuttered. "W-what do you mea-"

Tuppy nodded, and Reina sprung forward, grabbing his shoulder.

In a second, in a heart-stopping instant, he was gone.

Reina's face, screwed up with effort, immediately melted with exhaustion as her knees gave out. Tuppy moved to help her, but Reina shook her head. "I'm fine, go check on Ethan."

Tuppy glanced back to the fountain, pain and confusion warping her thoughts. "Check on..."

There, where he'd collapsed, Ethan was struggling to sit.

"Ethan...?" her words trailed off as she hurried to his side. Nua was already there, bracing him as he pulled himself up.

"Ow," he grunted, touching the place where his forehead had smashed into the ground.

Tuppy gaped in astonishment. "But... you were shot! I saw him shoot you—"

Ethan glanced down at his chest. His shirt was torn in the front and back—where the bullet had gone through, Tuppy realized with a roll of horror—but there was no blood. He wasn't bleeding.

He didn't die.

"Yeah, that kinda stings too," he said, wincing.

Reina made her way over, sinking to the ground beside Ethan. "You didn't have to do that, you know," she said, the reprimand softened by the relief and affection in her voice.

"Of course I did." He looked at Tuppy earnestly. "I was so scared he was going to kill you. But trust me, this isn't the worst I've had."

Tuppy's gut tightened, and her vision became foggy with tears. Reina's words from yesterday seemed to echo around her: *He was half-dead when we found him. Beaten within an inch of his life.*

"You can't die?"

He let out a tiny snort, then coughed. "Pretty damn sure I can, just not from... you know."

"Violence," Reina finished for him. She opened her arms to Nua, who shuffled closer and allowed herself to be enveloped. Reina stroked her hair as the girl sniffled. "I'm sorry you had to see that, sweetie."

Nua turned her head to look back at Ethan, furiously signing something at him.

He let out a wet little sigh. "I promise I won't. Not unless I absolutely have to."

Tuppy met Reina's eye, the same unspoken understanding flickering between them as it had before. "Thank you," Tuppy said, though the words could never be enough. "For coming back, and for—" she couldn't say it.

"I was halfway to the van when I heard," Reina said. "God, I am so, so proud of you, Tuppy—that was so fucking brave."

"Well, I—" Tuppy glanced at Nua and Ethan and then back. "I had some help." She swallowed past a tight throat. "Thank you. For... for saving me."

"No," Reina shook her head, giving Tuppy a tired smile. "You saved yourself the night you left."

They huddled together at the base of the fountain until dawn. Deciding once and for all that it was time to get out of the park, Ethan led the way back to the van.

After stopping at an all-night diner to pick up breakfast, Tuppy munched on a bagel as they sat in the parking lot overlooking the harbor, watching as the sunrise broke over the horizon.

"I was thinking maybe the suburbs?" Ethan suggested, rolling his trash wrapper into a ball and chucking it at Nua, who caught it easily and launched it back at him with a giggle. "Might be nice to get away from everything for a while." He glanced at Tuppy. "What do you think, Ms. Tuppy?"

"I'd love to get out of the city," she admitted, taking another deep breath of the fresh air wafting in over the water. A cloud of peace drifted over her, unfamiliar but inviting. "I haven't been traveling since—oh dear, it's been decades."

Reina drained the rest of her four–espresso shot latte and unfurled the map she'd laid on her lap. "I'm down. Where should we go, Nua?"

Nua's legs stopped swinging on the bench, her eyes growing glassy and distant.

She called it flying, Tuppy remembered. And watching the girl, her dark hair caressing her face as it blew in the wind, her tiny body still and undisturbed, that was truly what it looked like.

They waited several minutes before Nua jolted into awareness. She wasn't shaking with panic like the last time, but she still reached for Ethan's hand, her breath tight and eyes wide.

"It's alright, dear," Tuppy said, hoping that her voice would soothe the child's distress. "It's alright, we're here, you're safe."

Nua blinked several times, then hurried to explain, her little hands moving faster than Tuppy could process.

"She saw someone," Ethan explained, squeezing Nua's shoulder. "There's a girl in trouble, a couple miles from here..."

"Swan's Dive bridge," Reina said as Nua concluded the details of her vision. She quickly refolded the map. "I know where that is. If I drive, we can get there in less than ten."

Ethan huffed in mock-offense. "I feel personally attacked, somehow."

Tuppy leaned in to Nua as they all stood, heading back to the van. "You did great," she praised.

Nua smiled, slipping one hand into Tuppy's and using her other to touch her chin, signing something that even Tuppy could recognize: *Thank you.*

"Now," Tuppy said, staring into the distance, towards Swan's Dive bridge, "let's go find her."

A Handful of Mud

Artyv K

Artyv K lives in the land of the raging sun and figures a time might come when Helios might either bake us all or outright disappear. At this moment, she thinks the odds are evenly matched.

It's late in the afternoon when *mipaati* skulks in, her eyes still carrying the gunk from yesterday and her face sunken with a fidgety anxiousness for tomorrow. Her appearance—bedraggled and nervous—lends a sense of foreboding to the proceedings. Mtra and I watch our grandmother guardedly as she shuts the door behind her and scurries inside our patched walls, holding a lump in the hem of her saree. Her georgette is frayed at the edges; it's a navy-blue relic, a memento from her former life as a Tupperware hustler, one she's always telling stories about. She is an unapologetic hoarder, our *mipaati*, and I've often held a lingering suspicion that she picked us from the dumps too, that we're perhaps yet another part of her hoard. Today is all about the lump though; she cradles it with the tenderness reserved for a newborn and ushers us into a corner. My sister and I comply, for the hush of the affair excites us, its mystery and suspense spurring us on to partake in her secrecy. For once in our lives, we are glad to follow her cue. For once in our lives, we feel thrilled to do something that isn't nothing. It beats counting bars on the fencing outside camp; it beats playing hopscotch with whittled down chalk; and it certainly beats memorizing timetables for trains we can always hear but never see. I wonder if *mipaati* has finally grown into the mold of a responsible adult and found us some food.

How wrong was I.

Grandma steps forward, her eyes darting around in search of a container to dump her secret in. She ventures to her hoarder heap and fetches a take-out box from the top of the pile, giving the thing a thorough look. Meanwhile Mtra's patience runs the end of its course, and she grows restless from all the subterfuge. "Is it chocolate? It's chocolate, isn't it?" my six-year-old sister demands of *mipaati*, dogging the old woman at every turn and footstep while sniffing out the hem of her saree.

Mipaati humors my sister with a smile.

"No, it's even *better*," she insists, her grey eyes gleaming.

We watch as she unrolls the *pallu* of her saree and dumps her spoils into the container.

There's a silence— a long, hard silence. I stare at the tribute on our table; I recognize the thing for what it is and my eyes widen a little.

"Is that mu—?" I barely manage to utter before a hand clamps around my mouth.

Mipaati gasps in horror, muffling my question before I can even speak it.

"*Sshh*, you idiot," she hisses furiously and gives a frantic look around. Her eyes scan the walls of our dwelling, roving from corner to corner; she looks uneasy and so very afraid. She waits for voices to break out or a door to slam open and when nothing happens, she turns to me. *Don't call it out loud,* she reproaches me in a whisper. *Walls have ears, remember?* She hazards a look at the door again and when no one's outside, banging it open, her nerves lose their edge, and she sags back into her wrinkled skin, looking relieved. She doesn't release me yet. No, not until I bite my tongue and promise to treat the subject of her spoils with more delicacy.

"But *mipaati*," I protest in a small voice. "How—" My face betrays my chagrin, knowing she is up to her foolish schemes again. "Where did you even get this?"

The old fossil shrugs and evades the question.

"Never you mind," she replies tartly. "It took some persuasion. Took some bartering as well. But my pains will bear fruit; just wait and watch, my dove."

Mtra, never one to be left out of a conversation, presses her elbows on the table and leans her small head in.

"Is that mud?" she asks belligerently, earning another furious squawk from our grandmother.

"The walls. THE WALLS!" *mipaati* bemoans.

Undeterred, my sister merely grins and drops her voice to a whisper. "But what can you do with a handful of mud, granny?"

Our *mipaati* turns to the walls again and scorns at them.

"We can do so much, gumdrop. Mud is versatile like life itself. It gives and it takes."

Truer words have been spoken.

"Like what?" I ask, raising the voice of the skeptic.

Mipaati isn't insulted by my query. She glances at me, this time with a strange fervor in her eyes, like a missionary come to educate the savages.

"We can make new life, Dana. Plant a tree, a shrub, even grow *food*," her voice thrums with energy, enthused at the myriad possibilities before her. "It will be like living above ground. Just like old times, children."

My sister tugs at our grandmother's elbow.

"How about chocolates? Can we grow chocolates, *mipaati*?"

Our grandmother's face turns sour. She shakes her head mutedly.

"No, we won't," she vows. "Chocolates are symbols of capitalism, a means to slavery, Mtra. It's the reason why we can't live above anymore. All because of industrialists and their bottomless greed! The corrupt are the ones who ruined everything! We were happy back then!"

If it isn't apparent already, *mipaati* is a stout proponent of alternative theories. Especially those derived from tabloids she scavenges out of dumpsters. I wouldn't exactly call her a socialist since she doesn't like sharing much, least of all her after-meal mango puddings. My sister's enthusiasm deflates a little, and our grandmother, noticing the lull in her spirit, reaches out to pet Mtra's head, smoothing out the tangles in her black hair. "Don't be disheartened, dove," she tells Mtra and after a long moment of deliberation, she concedes a sigh. "Know what? Perhaps we can *try* growing chocolates too. But don't get your hopes up, alright?"

Mtra perks up immediately while *mipaati* turns to the table to gaze ardently at her spoils. Her eyes blaze like wildfire.

I look between the two of them—between guardian and ward—knowing not the fool between them. I step away, hoping their delusions aren't infectious.

***

Let it not be said that I didn't try. The presence of mud in our room keeps me on edge and nags at me throughout the day. During dinner of mashed potatoes and lemon rice (which arrived, wrapped in banana leaves and coir strings, thanks to government food stamps and the biodegradable initiative), I clear my throat and offer a suggestion—a suggestion that ought to be more practical than the schemes grandma concocts inside her head.

"*Mipaati*," I call. "How about we turn the mud into clay? We can make something out of it."

My grandmother clicks her tongue, turning down the idea.

I propose another.

"How about we use it to seal the crack in our roof? Remember that corner over the heater and how it drips every time it rains?"

Mipaati shakes her head again, her answer another stout 'no'.

"We are going to grow our own food," she says determinedly. "— and that is final."

"But—" I protest, wondering if she's even thinking straight. "What about water? What about seeds?"

Her attention draws to the crude calendar we have marked on the wall. Letters from Sunday to Saturday and a number to go with each day. *Mipaati* ruminates over the calendar before turning to me. "Tomorrow will be gourd" she says, remembering the schedule of rations and food distributed by State Relief Housing. "If you find some seeds in your curry tomorrow, spit them out, alright?"

I stare at her, shell-shocked, amazed that she's intent on going through with this.

"What about *light*?" I blurt out.

Here, she pauses, finding herself to be at a loss for words. She glances around our home, our cantonment home, and grows dismayed at the state of it. Shadows cling to the inside of our dwelling; there's no light except for the fluorescent tube glowing outside the cantonment and attracting the moths. I'm surprised how she even missed such a crucial detail.

"I'll... I'll figure out something," she says.

I'm not convinced.

It's an irony how my grandmother—the plastic toting jezebel of yesterday—has turned into a tree hugger. I wonder if she's prepared to handle the gravity of this change.

***

Our grandmother keeps the mud in its makeshift pot, away from prying eyes. She's planted something in there. I don't know what it is.

You must excuse me for the little faith I place in my guardian. For my grandmother is as strange as they come, her stories stranger than her. It's *mipaati's* habit to share euphemisms during laundry. Mtra and I are sitting on the ground, elbows drawn around our grubby knees, faces burrowed in our hands while the drums spin. Mtra watches on in awe, enamored by the machines and the *chug-chug* rhythm of their spin cycles. There's no ventilation in the cantonment's laundry room, and we nearly bake in the heat of twenty machines chugging dirt and filth.

Mipaati speaks up suddenly.

"Don't ever ask questions to a drowning man," grandmother tells us sagely.

We look up at her, startled.

Mipaati doesn't give reason and continues folding linen in her lap. Against my better judgment, I clear my throat and ask her what she means. Grandma glances at me sharp as if the answer ought to be obvious.

"Because if you ask questions to a drowning man, and if he drowns, you'd blame no one but yourself."

I stare at her, confounded. We don't get it, really. Neither me nor my sister understand what she's on about. Why anyone would court death by drowning? Or why we'd be shooting questions to a drowning man and not be saving him instead? We'd never learnt how to swim either—my sister and I. We've never seen a pool or the sea. We can imagine how it must feel; after all, we've seen ads in the ol' magazines, a poster of a woman in a bikini, lying flat on top of a turtle float, drinking from a glass that has a little umbrella and a slice of cucumber. I called dibs on the umbrella while Mtra announced her rights to the slice of cucumber. So, that's the extent of what we know about pools, swimming and how to float and drown in them. We return to watching our grandmother; we watch her haul our clothes out of the laundromat; and we follow her out to the subterra yard where she hooks the clothes on a line to dry. *Mipaati* says the clothes would dry quicker if the sun were here. Or if the dryer wasn't kept out of order to conserve electricity. Another reason why *mipaati* isn't fond of capitalism or the machines. She's eager to return home, to her handful of mud.

My sister and I are content to watch the clothes dry, because we have time, all the time in the world, and because somebody might just steal our clothes if we don't keep that watch.

Somewhere, in the back of my mind, I entertain a hope that somebody would steal the mud.

But it's still there when we get back.

***

The next day, *mipaati* is running late from her errands, and I wonder if they caught her.

The sentinels.

The quarantiners.

Will they come for us next?

I drag Mtra away from home, paranoia digging its claws deep in me.

The gayatri mantra bounces off the sound bar over tin homes and in other places—someone's playing the old songs of MGR. The people of the underground still believe in their gods, in their heroes, and are still waiting for their day of reckoning. Their day of the sun. There is a buzz of static, and the songs are broken by a metro announcement.

I clutch my sister's hand in mine and navigate through the tunnels. There are ventilator shafts at every twenty steps, bringing in recycled air, ribbons dancing under them.

Mtra drags her feet, wanting to stay under the airy shafts.

"Where are we going? Where is *mipaati*?" she whines.

I try to pull her along with force.

"C'mon, walk," I urge her. "I don't know where the old crone is, alright. She said she's going to get some torchlights from the commissary."

Mtra yanks her arm free and whimpers.

"Then, lets head back home and wait. She'll come back, won't she?"

I turn to my sister and reach for her hand again, afraid to let her go. "Mtra, trust me, will you?" I tell her, but she doesn't believe a word of mine. I look at the tunnel, at the great unknown beyond and wonder if it's easier to trust in my foolish grandmother than me.

We hear a thunderous echo next.

"It's the train," says my sister, growing buoyant. We feel it rumbling down the network of subway tunnels.

Mtra looks at me.

"Do you think it's true?"

"What?"

"That the train is carried by the Whistling Man. That's where the sound comes from?"

I scowl.

"Who told you that?"

"*Mipaati.*"

I sigh and sink to my knees, grasping hold of her shoulders.

"Mtra, don't believe everything *mipaati* says. You can't... trust her."

My sister looks puzzled.

"Does this mean we can't grow chocolate too?"

***

Mipaati returns at the crack of dawn. We know because Srini's roosters are crowing already, the little beasts. Our grandmother can hardly contain her excitement and I understand why. She's siphoned off a pair of flashlights from somewhere.

I'm tempted to ask if she stole them from the commissary.

Humming to herself a song, she sets about fixing the flashlights around her box of mud.

"What makes you think it's safe?" I finally ask her, rubbing the sleep out of my eyes. "What makes you think your mud isn't poisoned like the land above?"

Mipaati throws me a peeved look.

"Of course, it isn't poisoned. Don't be ridiculous, Dana."

I'm not convinced. I don't know what she's planted in there, but one day we see the seed germinating. Just a pair of leaves pops out, tiny, miniscule, and it takes both Mtra and me to hold back our grandmother and muffle her cries of jubilation. After a week, more leaves join the fray and the plant looks like a basil now, because that's the only plant I've seen growing underground.

I don't tell my sister—my sister who still thinks the plant is going to sprout chocolate bars one day.

***

The plant grows into a sapling and as it grows, *mipaati* becomes obsessed with it. She sacrifices her tea to the sapling, prays to it, tells it all her strange stories. It occurs to *mipaati* one day that the plant is in dire need of mulch. It occurs to *mipaati* that we possess neither pebbles nor wooden chips to achieve this feat.

It's not until Mtra and I are breaking our midday eggs (from the government's an egg a day programme) that I look up and catch the fervent expression on grandmother's face. Mtra willingly gives up her egg, but I shake my head, denying her silent plea.

"No!" I grit.

"Just the shell, it's good for the soil."

"It's good for me too," I insist, protecting my egg shells.

I give the woman a scathing look. The only reason she keeps us around is for the government food stamps, I'm sure.

Mipaati purses her lips in a thin line. I know she'll have her way, and I try to barter.

"Then tell me, what happened to our parents?"

Grandma groans.

"Haven't we had this discussion already? It was tuberculosis."

"You said they died in a car crash!"

Mipaati turns irritated.

"Look at you. Remembering stuff. You're just a kid, act your age."

Our grandmother flip-flops between asking us to act like adults and kids. It's almost as if she doesn't know what she wants us to be.

I sacrifice the egg shells anyway.

***

Our fears take shape on the tenth night when there's a knock on the door. *Mipaati* opens the door and falls back with a yelp; there's a crack of a taser and two hazmat suits restrain her with force while a third comes for Mtra and me.

"Are the kids compromised? Check them for toxicity!"

The hazmat suits scan us from head to toe, running our stats in their machines before declaring us 'clean'. Our grandmother doesn't go down without a fight; she bites into the hand of the officer holding her back. "We have rights!" she screams, struggling against him. "You can't barge in here!"

The sentinel growls back at her.

"We can if you are foolish enough to bring hazardous substances down. Where is it? WHERE?"

She simmers down and regards the hazmats with distrust.

"I don't know what you're talking about," she snarls.

"For the last time, where is it, you blithering old fool?"

When *mipaati* isn't forthcoming with answers, the hazmat suits turn to us, the kids.

"Where is the soil, children? Do you know about it?"

Mtra lets out a sob and hides behind the cot, and so the responders turn to me. I give my grandmother a cold, hard look and then raising a hand, point to the chest of drawers.

The responders discover it soon enough.

"Is it mud?"

"Yes."

"Positive?"

"Yes."

"Good heavens."

The hazmat suits crowd around the box of mud. They rip away the plant, toss it to the floor and trample all over it with their boots. It's the mud they've come for, and they hold their breath as they scoop it into a ziplock bag with careful hands.

Exchanging wary glances, they scan the bag.

After what seems like a lifetime, the machine completes its tests and its display beeps green; there's a collective sigh of relief.

"False alarm," one hazmat announces. "Thank god."

They remove the 'Quarantine' sticker from our door and stick a 'Safe' over it. They leave, but not before slapping a two thousand rupee fine on *mipaati* for her audacity to smuggle mud, toxic or otherwise. When they're gone, all that's left is the circle of spectators standing outside our door. *Mipaati* is frozen to her spot, looking shell-shocked, her eyes glued to the floor and the remains of the plant.

I watch my sister crawl out of hiding. She stumbles over to the crushed basil, picks out a leaf and takes a bite. She pulls a face at the taste.

"This isn't chocolate," she says.

The Curse of Apollo

Diana Hurlburt

Diana daylights as a public librarian
on the sunny Gulf Coast (graduating
from the University of South
Florida's English and library science
programs put an official stamp on
what everyone already knew). When
not dispensing readers' advisory and
youth programs, she divides her
writing time between contemporary
romance and weird regional tales.
She has a soft spot for f/f, but loves
exploring queer friendships, families,
and other relationships in her stories.
An admitted place obsessive, she's
Florida-born and bred, but lived in
Cleveland for a time and left part of
her heart behind.

For each season there is a story. Some are more popular than others; Markos points out with a sly chuckle my expression of long-suffering when it is lambing time once more and someone begs for the tale of the boy Liberator among the king's flocks. At any rate, tales are a more pleasant way of counting the seasons than taxes, and a few tales become so well-loved that their beginnings twine with those of the rituals they celebrate, with no endings in sight.

So it went with the story of Kharis and the Day-Maker's keles.

Sometime between dark-sparking midnight and rosy-fingered dawn, late in the month of Poseideon, a foal was born among the herds of Lykosoura. This was as usual, for the Horse Lord's month is favored by those who breed mares, the god being close at hand to oversee his business. A bare six weeks later, early in the month of Elaphebolion, another foal was born, its passage into the world eased by the hand of the Huntress, who also watches over children of all kinds.

These occurrences would have passed without note had not the two foals been born of the same mare.

Now twins are sacred in that part of the country, but twin horses are rarely seen, and furthermore no one had ever heard of twins separated by such a lapse in their births. The people were unsure how to proceed. Some called for the sacrifice of both foals, one for each of the altars of the deities in question. Few had ever come to harm by being too careful of gods, after all. Some argued that the foals were themselves deities in disguise, come to Earth for a time to observe and learn, and thus should be treated better than any king. Some scoffed and held forth that they were only foals, after all—see, the red one kicks her heels in a foolish manner, and the gray has fallen into the trough in his eagerness to follow his mother—and belonged in the pasture with the mare, where they would learn to be horses like all others.

The conversation grew and swelled and broke only to rise again, much as the waves cresting on Lykosoura's southern shore.

Talk carries, and gossip moves as quickly as gold-fletched arrows. The Day-Maker's ravens ventured into that god's morning room, chattering of twins and deities and sacrifices, and his interest was piqued. Interest turned quickly to insult, for was he not also a twin? His sister the Huntress was one half of something greater, neither of them whole without the other, and the matter of these twin foals could not be resolved without consulting him. Yet the people of Lykosoura seemed to have forgotten this: none had sent to his oracle high in the mountains above the countryside, and his devotees in the city's temple remained overlooked while those of the Huntress and Horse Lord scurried and ferreted in their archives and fretted. The Day-Maker's mood grew stormy, and clouds passed over the sun as the people continued their debate.

That evening, after the people had taken to bed still murmuring over the spring's strange events, a shadow moved across the pasture.

"A blight?" said old Kharis, chief keeper of the village's horses, when she gazed over the fence in the morning. The grass was as she'd left it, and the rambling pines to the north as bitterly green as always, and the twenty-odd horses turned out milling and browsing about their affairs. But one of the new foals, the gray, had undergone some change: his shining pale coat was now black. Not darkest bay, nor deep earthy liver, but true black, as though his hair had been stripped away to reveal the night-colored skin beneath.

The copper filly appeared her foolish self, though Kharis felt a strange inclination to take her from her mother—wean her on pine liquor, perhaps, or chicken feed. It was quite clear that the filly could not be trusted to know her own mind.

The sight of the now-black colt startled Kharis, so that she retreated to the Liberator's temple to seek the herbalists' advice.

Lykosoura is a staid country, its temperament stemming, people say, from the rocks on which it grows. Though the inhabitants are dutiful to their gods, even devoted, they do not often fall into superstition. In this case, frugality won out. The sacrifice of two hardy foals, even strange ones, seemed ludicrous, an abject refusal of the gods' gifts. Two lambs were brought to the altars of the Huntress and the Horse Lord instead, with all proper rites and adornments. The foals were left with their mother, who was a very good mare, to learn to be horses. And if people looked askance at the pair, whispered about the colt's new, black-singed coat—

Two years passed.

In the month of Thargelion, on the sixth and seventh days, a festival was held celebrating the birth of the Divine Twins. The Huntress was lauded with a procession through the trees, her beacon lit on the tallest crag above Lykosoura as twilight melted into night and the moon rose in its slenderest crescent.

Deer were slain and roasted, the goodness and wisdom of the goddess saluted with wine, and hunters brought their bows and knives and hounds to be blessed alongside the youngest children. On the following morning, while night gave way to dawn, a race would be held, to honor the Day-Maker's horses when they drew the sun across the firmament.

This was the most hotly-contested race throughout the countryside; from every hamlet tucked into the hills people came, bringing their best horses to be tried upon a course that ranged from the lowland grasses through steepening rocks and ended at a spring nestled between peaks, where the god's most sacred shrine was housed.

Each horse entered was the pride of its household or village. Folk trained up their runners from the first days of their birth, if the foal looked likely, and on the festival day each horse was groomed until it shone, manes braided with fine ribbons and tails lifted high as banners. All along the path to Lykosoura's temple block, people admired the horses and compared their beauty to what was said of their skill, for the Day-Maker's race was no place to test an unbroken steed, a rank stallion, a flighty youngster. It was understood, though rarely stated, that this was the test of horses already proven. It was dangerous and long, requiring speed and dexterity and wind as deep as the caverns of Khthonos. The winners each year were the ideal union of horse and rider, verging on demigods and creatures of myth, and were crowned at the god's spring with his laurels. Since the race's first running, its victors had produced war-steeds, the mounts of kings, and–so it was murmured–the winged horse of Hodios, upon whom the business of the gods traveled more swiftly than sunlight and more smoothly than running water.

To such a race did old Kharis lead a pair of half-wild young horses.

Lykosoura is close to the heavens, and as such inhabits a space where the veil between worlds is thin. To live in a place like that requires a sense of humor, which Kharis had in spades. What need had she for laurels and acclaim, at her advanced age? She had delivered baby horses since the age of twelve, had seen every iteration of equine beauty and folly, had wept over foals choked by their birthing-bags and breech hooves and colic. She was hale yet; she went along on the autumn's wolf-hunt and rode each morning, and there was nothing in the by-laws governing the Day-Maker's race, the keles of heroes, to prevent her horses from running, nor her from riding.

"What!" people said along the main thoroughfare, lined up with torches and lanterns to watch the horses proceed. "Kharis, old woman, you aim to ride them both?"

Kharis smiled, a hand on either horse's muzzle, for neither reins nor saddles were permitted in the race, and the people's laughter drained away to whispers. No one could deny that the twin horses looked likely: they had grown up large and fine, well-muscled, haughty-browed. The colt's black coat gleamed as though oiled, and the red filly flirted her tail, which whipped like copper wire. It was known that many had attempted to ride the filly and that no one, even Kharis, had ever been seen aboard her. It was known also that the colt was believed cursed, for the matter of his coat shifting color had never been forgotten. Few people ventured near them in the pasture or stables, and fewer still asked after their health and training, and no one at all had ever offered to buy them.

"Well," said Iakolanthus, and shook his coin purse. "It's a bet only a trickster would make."

Some people could not resist such bets, and some of those are gods. In his high places, the Day-Maker's attention was caught and he peered down to see his images celebrated.

The horses lined up at the gate of the Day-Maker's temple in the heart of Lykosoura, snorting and pawing the raked sand as they and their riders were blessed. The priests paused when they reached Kharis and her pair, but soon enough hands moved over the aged woman's head and the horses' dainty muzzles, words murmured in ritual to keep hooves sound and arms strong. Kharis fixed her eyes on the horizon, still gray with night. The peaks of Lykosoura pierced the dark sky, cradling the Day-Maker's spring close and hidden, and the pathway snaked out in front of her, and it seemed that the sand spoke to her as it did the horses, whispering of its depth and hardness, raked and packed tight for hooves to run upon.

The riders were ready when a deep bell chimed and their mounts burst forward. All along the thoroughfare, the people of Lykosoura exclaimed, pointing and clutching one another, at the sight of Kharis balanced between the twin runners.

(Markos likes to joke, gruffly, that none shall ever see his hoplite armor aboard a horse and why should they, when Kharis can manage the whole cavalry at once?)

It was remembered, suddenly, that Kharis had been born on the plains to Lykosoura's west, one of the horsewomen who trained mounts for battle and for mirth. It was said those women were born of mares themselves, daughters of the great mare sprung from the Horse Lord's white-crested wave, the offspring of land and sea. They held the secrets of breeding runners and massive draft beasts and fine-boned ponies for princesses, and on a girl's twelfth birthday she was given a brew of fermented colostrum and blood and sent out to gentle a yearling.

Given everything the people had heard of the plains women, Kharis did not seem so strange.

The colt and filly galloped strongly, even and matched in their strides, one of Kharis's feet planted on each of their backs. She was half-crouched, fingers wrapped in their manes, steady as any of the statues on the Day-Maker's temple porch. It did not matter that the twin horses had had no opportunity to race prior, that the people believed they were rank and feral. She had watched them and worked with them and talked to them, and she knew what she was about.

The colt's strange coat was no fault of his; Kharis recognized the hand of a god when she saw it. He couldn't help the darkening of his flanks and throat, any more than Kharis could help the curl of her hair or the fingers of her left hand, three of which had grown together in the womb and never separated after birth. The filly's temperament was something to be worked with, rather than beaten away. She had a contrary way about her, such that an observer was inclined to ignore all signs the filly gave, and try their own ideas. Kharis resisted this and believed the filly when she indicated that she was hungry, or sore, or—as now—that she could run faster than Kharis had previously believed.

"Well then," she called to the filly, and the colt picked up his heels with them.

They ran, the race's path curving through the town and fields, growing rough underfoot when it entered the woods. The other horses frothed beside them, or fell behind, stumbled on stones not removed from the track, tossed their heads sideways to try and savage their fellows. Riders cursed at one another, pleaded with the gods, fell in exhaustion or were thrown. The joints of Kharis's knees ached, but the sharp spring wind teased hair loose from her braid and nipped her cheeks, and she decided that she had never felt better. Whatever the origins of her horses, she loved their mother. It wasn't the mare's fault that her delivery had been a little faulty, and they had both done as good a job as they knew, raising the twins. No matter if they won the Day-Maker's race, or if they were declared illicit upon winning, since to her knowledge only one horse was permitted the victory.

They were running, according to the manner of their making.

The air thinned and chilled as the race wound through Lykosoura's mountains, and the horses' breath fogged the path. Kharis noted that the other runners had lagged behind–or perhaps she and the twins were already beaten, and one of the other horses now knelt at the spring, draped in laurel and trodding palm underfoot. But no: the sun was inching above the peaks, and if they ran just a bit further, just a touch swifter, they would reach it. Within her breast, Kharis's heart fluttered like a captive bird. Glory suffused her skin, her body warming as sunlight spread over the mountains. Beneath her feet the horses were warm, sweat-lathered, steam rising from their withers to match their clouds of breath. The rhythm of their hooves pounding the earth changed; no longer did the harsh impact ripple up into Kharis from below, and it seemed to Kharis that they rose, the three of them, the mountainside dropping away and the horses' breath disappearing into thick clouds scudding through the sky.

"Well." The voice was pleased, whoever it belonged to. Kharis had thought she knew the priesthood serving the Day-Maker at his spring, but this voice was unfamiliar, deep and bell-like, amused. "Do you seek to usurp my position, child?"

She had not been a child for long years.

"I seek nothing but the spring," Kharis said. She slid down

between the twins as the horses stilled, squinting into a scarlet dawn. "They have proved themselves, I should think, these two."

"They have brought the sun," the Day-Maker said, "and my own pair still dozing in their stable." He laughed. "I would be half-inclined to surrender the sun's business to such a set on the basis of a well-run keles." He petted the colt's nose, and his noble face broadened with laughter. "I remember you. How shall I forget you, with the mark of my hand upon you?" The filly whickered and tossed her wet mane, and the god nodded to her. "And you, mistress. Reminiscent of another stubborn woman of my acquaintance. It is only right that you should torment your brother, and inspire his best."

Kharis knelt, which was relief to her joints. "The sun's business was not my intention, my lord. We had only a race to run." She hesitated, glancing toward where she expected to see the holy spring and its keepers. There was only a haze, red as the filly's coat and shot through with darts of light. "Have the other horses ended where they ought?"

"What care have I for other horses?" The god studied Kharis. His eyes were startling, the searing white-gold of hottest noon. "These two have proven themselves worthier than any since Bellerophon's steed. They are yours, correct? May I have them?"

Kharis faltered. Nothing in her raising had taught her to refuse a god. All women knew the results of the Day-Maker's annoyance.

"They are mine inasmuch as a horse is ever a human's." She laid a hand on the colt's belly, and the other on the filly's, where the breath of each horse was beginning to slow. "They do as they will. The filly especially."

"A good and holy appraisal," the Day-Maker said. "I admire

them, but the admiration of gods is not so specific as the love of humans. A mile wide, rather than a fathom deep. It is right they remain with you, and you with them." A crafty smile crossed his lips. "Some slight recollection of debts owed comes to mind, and I hate to be in debt."

Each word ground on Kharis's senses. The roots of her hair ached. She began to feel as though she was slowly being dismantled, piece by piece. The horses remained unperturbed. "I know of no debt, my lord."

"A petty thing and a hasty one." Some reluctant apology entered the god's voice, which Kharis would have chuckled over in wonder had she not been concentrating on staying upright in his presence. "It is no fault of these two, how their birth was received by humans, and you did well by them when others would not."

Kharis bowed her head, sweat springing at her temples. She wanted to be gone from that place. Exhaustion drilled through her bones. What more was there waiting for her, in Lykosoura below, when she had ridden two horses to the solar palace?

"Perhaps you and they have not come to take over the sun's business," the Day-Maker said, "but still you belong in the heavens."

So it was that Kharis and the twins entered the skies above Lykosoura: accidentally, bearing the sun to its master between them, and then purposefully, Kharis's white hair bright between the bloody copper of the filly and the coal-fired black of the colt. They went to the stars in a tight cluster and were called the Dromeades ever after, the runners; they who appear as night drains away, the harbingers of daybreak, the Horses of the Sun.

Wise Woman

Regina Higgins

Regina Higgins has written stories published at Everyday Fiction and Rainbow Rumpus. She's also the author of Magic Kingdoms, a book about classic children's literature, published by Simon & Schuster. She lives in Lexington, Kentucky, with her husband and is writing a novel.

Ever since I was a child I'd been to Mildred for anything you can name—drops for toothache, herbs to ward off hoof-and-mouth (you fasten them on the off hind leg with a special knot), and readings, of course. A couple of years ago, she told me I'd have a child before the next spring, and it happened, alright. Only one of the eight cousins to give birth so far, and I'm the youngest. My mother and aunts had just about given up hope of a baby in the family. It's the way of things now, since the war and all the problems with the air and water.

Maybe Mildred helped it along—threw in a little something extra, since she knew I wanted a child. If anyone could do it, it was Mildred. She'd been practicing for over seventy years. It's forbidden, of course. The Council decided the wise women can foretell birth, but they can't bring it about by spells. That was their one and only attempt to assert control. And the penalty for defying the Council's order is death.

But Mildred wasn't one for following rules she thought were silly, especially if it stood in the way of her helping someone. She was just like that.

There's a saying in town, you find your wise woman and only then will you find your true love. But Mildred and I go back long before I had any thoughts of love at all. She put a special charm on my first bicycle. And I never had an accident with it after that. My cousin Sylvia, now, she went to Agnes for spells, and her bicycle frame was warped in four months. That was two months longer than her marriage lasted. I had better luck with Mildred, who pointed out Tom and said he'd be a good match for me. She was right. So I've stuck with Mildred.

I was on my way to her house when I heard about the whole business. I had James in the stroller—ten months old, I think he was—and we were enjoying the early autumn breeze, walking out to the edge of town, beyond the old power station, where Mildred's cottage was set way back from the road.

We were in the part of town where the officers' housing left over from the war had been remade for families when I heard some-one call me. It was my cousin Sylvia, and she was waving to me from her porch, the one Tom fixed up for her after her mother died. When I looked up at her, she waved frantically for me to come closer.

"We're on the way to Mildred's," I told her as I wheeled the stroller up the flagstone path.

Sylvia rushed down the steps at that. "I know, Charlotte," she said. "That's why I called you." She lifted the front end of the stroller. "Come on in, I've got something to tell you."

"Can't we sit on the porch?" To tell the truth, I never much liked the inside of my aunt's house. She'd kept it dark and cluttered it with her many incomplete projects—piles of quilt squares and rolls of material for dresses that never quite got done.

Sylvia shook her head. "It's private."

I looked around at the empty street, the quiet houses. "Who'll hear us?"

She sat down, but drew my chair very close, so our knees were almost touching.

"It's about Mildred," she whispered.

"What is?"

Sylvia pressed her lips together and took a deep breath before speaking. "It's—she's been accused."

"Of what?"

"Of casting a birth spell. For—" she pointed to James, who was dozing in the stroller. "They're not supposed to do that, you know."

I sat up straighter. "I know the rules, Sylvia, and so does Mildred. What's their proof?"

"Oh, there's no proof. Not yet. She's just been accused."

"And how did this happen?" I could feel the warm blood rushing to my face.

"Well, I shouldn't say . . . "

I waited. When Sylvia said that it meant she couldn't wait to spill the tea.

Sure enough, she leaned closer to me. "My Agnes made the complaint to the Council. Unfair competition, she called it."

I snorted. "So professional jealousy now constitutes proof of wrongdoing?"

"It's just an accusation," Sylvia insisted. "But that's enough, don't you think? To keep away from Mildred, just in case?"

I flinched at that. "Is it contagious?"

"Well, in a way." She shrugged. "You don't want trouble." Her eyes were on James in the stroller. "If they think it was you who asked for the spell . . . Or if you tell Mildred she's accused." She seized my arm. "You shouldn't tell. The accusation hearing is secret. If you tell, they'll—" She looked directly at James. "Well, you don't want to lose something—you know, that may be mixed up with Mildred."

I was on my feet. "Thanks for the information, Sylvia," I said as calmly as I could. Then I directed the stroller towards the steps and bumped it down by myself.

"Don't get involved, Charlotte!" she shouted after me.

I kept moving on the path and pushed the stroller down the street to Mildred's.

***

Mildred's cottage was small, made of stones her family had gathered for who knows how long ago. The garden had been tended by four generations of Mildred's family, and still produced the best vegetables in the area. They'd been the first family to build solar panels, even when the rest of the town had oil and gas to burn. "Just makes sense," they'd replied to those who'd laughed at their eccentricities. It was something Mildred herself often said.

Mildred saw Charlotte pushing James in the stroller through the trees towards her door that morning and turned to put on the kettle for tea. Out in the garden, she picked peppermint leaves and waited for her young friends.

Charlotte smiled as she approached. "Don't tell me you already know why I'm here."

Mildred laughed at that. "No, dear, I can't say I do. These leaves are for tea. But is it something in the garden you've come for? Tummy trouble? Teething?"

Charlotte kneeled beside the stroller. "He's doing well now. But the teeth coming in have been bothering him."

"Oh, yes. There must be a better way to grow teeth. Some chamomile, then." She reached over a hedge and picked some more leaves. "I'll prepare a tincture you can rub on the gums."

Once they were inside the cottage, Mildred placed the peppermint in a teapot and the chamomile in a small jar. She took the whistling teakettle off the stove and poured the water carefully into both.

"It should cool a bit. Before you leave, I'll show you how to apply it, dear. It really does help the poor little ones. Will you have some tea first?"

"Yes, please."

While Charlotte sat at the wooden table in the kitchen, Mildred gathered the cups. They were serviceable, but, it must be said, a bit lopsided. Still, Mildred loved them and used them proudly. She hid a grin and began her usual talk about them. "Do you know, these cups were made by a little girl who was just learning—"

"—just learning pottery," Charlotte chimed in. "I do, Mildred. It was me. And thank you."

"I treasure them. What a very serious little girl you were. Just ten, weren't you?" She poured the peppermint tea into the cups.

"I was, and you took me on as your student, although I think you had your doubts."

"Never." Mildred shook her head. She watched as Charlotte sipped her tea. She noticed that, although James was playing with his hands and making happy sounds, Charlotte was watching him with what looked like concern.

"Is there something else you need, dear?" Mildred asked.

Charlotte started at that, and put down her cup carefully. "Well, yes, I guess so."

"You seem just a bit distracted."

Charlotte bit her lip. "Could I have a reading?"

"Certainly, dear." Mildred put her cup aside and fished a deck of cards from the pocket of her apron. "Always have them at hand, just in case."

"Well, you're the best in town."

Mildred noted Charlotte's forced smile and began shuffling the deck. "And just what is the question? Or do you have one?"

"I do." Charlotte nodded.

"Full spread, or one card?"

"How about three cards?"

"Past, present, future." She placed the deck on the table. "And the question?"

"It's about a friend who may be in trouble," said Charlotte. "Can you tell me about it? What will happen?"

Mildred frowned. "I can tell you what *might* happen. No guarantees."

"But you told me I'd have a baby before the next spring, and you were right about that."

"Well, that was different. This may be more complicated. And," she looked right at Charlotte, "you're not giving me much information."

"No, I know," admitted Charlotte. "But can you still give me a reading?"

"Yes, of course." She placed a hand gently on Charlotte's forehead. "Just think about the person."

Charlotte drew back. "Why are you doing that?"

"It helps me, dear. Just think about the person, and we'll see about the danger."

Charlotte breathed out slowly as she closed her eyes. Mildred looked at her intently and kept a hand on her forehead. Then Mildred closed her eyes.

An old woman, stooped in her garden. She rises and greets a young girl who's crying, pulling an old bicycle. She'd fallen, badly gashed her knee, and come to the first house on the road. The old woman washes the knee carefully, offers the girl apple cider made from the trees out back. Before the girl leaves, the old woman sings a chant over the bicycle, wishes of safety and happiness.

"There." Mildred took her hand from Charlotte's forehead. "I'm ready now."

Mildred took up the deck and placed three cards on the table before her.

The Empress. The Emperor. The Tower.

"All Major Arcana," Mildred mused. "We're seeing some powerful possibilities here."

"Does that mean . . . "

"Well, let's see. The past is The Empress, power of nature and power to do. Present is The Emperor. That's more power over, and it tends to be a social, political power. And the future—"

Charlotte looked at the picture and gasped. The broken tower, struck by lightning, two terrified people falling to certain death.

"That's horrible," she whispered. "I wish now I hadn't asked."

"Well, not necessarily," Mildred told her. "It's an end, that's for sure. But nothing stays the same forever. All this means is there may be a sudden change."

"For my friend, you mean?"

"Possibly. Another way of looking at it in context would be that the past was ruled by a gentle, creative force. That was replaced by a sterner power, people wanting to dominate rather than create."

"Sounds like the Council."

"But the future may be destruction of the present order—the downfall of the dominators." She swept the cards back into the deck.

"Do you really think so?"

"That's my reading. Someone else may interpret the cards differently."

"But you're the best."

Mildred smiled and shrugged her shoulders.

"You did tell me I'd have a baby, and that happened." She frowned. "What cards told you that? I don't remember."

"That's because I did the reading while you were out in the garden, picking elderflower for your cold. You didn't ask about it when you were here, but I could tell you were wondering. So I did the reading myself."

"And what were the cards?"

Mildred looked through the deck and drew out three cards. "The Ace of Wands first," she said, "and that's an indication of a new venture." She placed the card before Charlotte, so she could see the image of the hand in a cloud, grasping a wand with blossoms on it.

"And then the Ten of Cups, domestic happiness." Charlotte saw the young couple, arms around each other under a rainbow of cups, their children dancing beside them.

"And last—and this is the most important, for me, at least— The Sun. That's the baby card, my dear. Birth before the next year. Always."

Charlotte smiled at the naked cherub riding the horse in the foreground, images of flowers under a beaming sun behind it.

"Look at them carefully, Charlotte. I'm serious, now. Really look at them."

As Charlotte looked at the cards, Mildred leaned over to James in the stroller. She picked him up and placed him gently on her lap.

"Sweet boy," she whispered. "Now I'll show your mama how to stop that bad, bad pain."

***

"The meeting will come to order."

The room fell silent, and the men on the dais looked down at their notes. The Council Chair, a balding man in his sixties, coughed and then spoke again.

"We convene this Extraordinary Meeting of the Council this evening to address a matter of some importance. "

A younger man to his right on the dais spoke up. "Point of order—"

"Yes?" the chair snapped.

"In characterizing the subject we're addressing this evening as 'a matter of some importance,' are we not implicitly saying that our usual discussion is not a matter of some importance?"

"No, we are not. Now let's get started before—"

"Shouldn't we then correct the record, sir? Rephrase the characterization? For the purpose of instructing future Council members, I really do think—"

"Let's just deal with this evening's business, sir. There's quite enough to do. Now, there's been a serious charge against one Mildred Cosgrove, who is accused of casting a birth spell. And I take it her accuser is here, but not the accused?" He lifted his glasses to check the hall.

"Mildred Cosgrove?" the Chair called out. "Please come forward."

No one responded.

"Let the record show, then, that the accused is not present," the Chair announced. "We may proceed. Now to the accuser. Agnes Reynaud? Please come forward."

Agnes stood and walked to the front of the room, before the assembled Council.

"Are you Agnes Reynaud?"

"I am, sir."

"And you accuse Mildred Cosgrove of casting a birth spell?"

"I do, sir."

The Chair folded his hands. "You realize this is a serious matter."

"I do, sir."

"You realize the penalty is death?"

Agnes nodded silently.

"You must speak, ma'am, so we can make your response part of the record," the younger man said.

The Chair turned with a withering glance to his right. Then he looked back to Agnes and nodded.

"I do realize the penalty is death, sir."

"Then state your case, ma'am."

Agnes turned so that the Council could see her. "About two

years ago, Mildred Cosgrove met with Charlotte. It was on herbal business."

"Could you explain that?"

"Charlotte wanted some herbs to cure a cold. But while she was there, she also had a reading. A reading of her future, to ask if she'd have a baby any time soon."

"And there's nothing wrong with that?"

"No, sir. Nothing wrong with foretelling the birth of a child. But—"

"But what? Speak up."

"Mildred cast a spell for Charlotte so a child would be born to her. It wasn't just a reading at all. It was a spell."

"And how do you know that, ma'am?"

Agnes cocked her head in annoyance at the question. "Well, the birth followed very quickly. She was suddenly with child practically that very month. And that's not the way of things now, is it?"

"It is suspicious, yes," the Chair conceded with a nod. "But couldn't it just be luck?"

Agnes drew herself up to her full height. "We in the craft know our business, sir. It's more than suspicious. It was deliberate."

"Was there a witness to this spell? Someone who could testify?"

She looked around the hall. "Only Charlotte, since Mildred's not here."

"Thank you, Agnes. You may step down now."

"But I haven't—"

"Thank you, ma'am. Charlotte Bellamy, are you present?"

Charlotte rose, handing James to her husband. She walked towards the front of the assembly, her legs trembling.

"Charlotte Bellamy," the Chair began, "you are called to witness in the case of Mildred Cosgrove, who is charged with casting a birth spell for you."

Charlotte threw a nervous glance back at Tom and James. "Yes, sir."

The younger man broke in. "In saying 'yes,' are you admitting she did indeed cast—"

"Sir, I will question the witness. Charlotte, calm yourself now. Did you ask Mildred to cast a birth spell for you?"

"No, sir, I didn't."

"But Mildred told you that you'd have a baby soon?"

"Yes, sir. Before the next spring," she said.

"And this was—when?"

"It was then spring, sir."

"So the prediction was correct? And there's nothing wrong with that, of course."

Agnes rose. "If I may, I should like to ask how Mildred predicted the birth."

The younger man turned to her with a frown. "Ma'am, you're out of order."

The Chair raised his hand. He nodded to Charlotte. "You may answer the question."

Charlotte grasped her hands to keep them from trembling. "It was a tarot reading."

Agnes smirked. "And what *exactly* were the cards?"

"Is this absolutely necessary?" the younger man asked, appearing exasperated. "I mean this kind of minutiae, should we concern ourselves with it?"

"What were the cards?" Agnes repeated.

Charlotte took a breath. "Ace of Wands, Ten of Cups, The Sun."

"Let me search her," Agnes said. She approached Charlotte and put a hand to her forehead.

An old woman at a table with a young woman, showing her the cards. The Ace of Wands, that's an indication of a new venture. The image of the hand in a cloud, grasping a wand with blossoms on it.

And the Ten of Cups, domestic happiness. A young couple, arms around each other under a rainbow of cups, their children dancing beside them.

And this is the most important, for me, at least—The Sun.

That's the baby card, my dear. Birth before the next year. Always.

Agnes drew back her hand. She lowered her head. "It's true. It's a true reading. I was wrong."

"Would you repeat that for the Council, Agnes?" said the Chair.

Agnes paused. "I withdraw my accusation."

"To be clear, ma'am . . . "

Agnes spoke loudly and deliberately. "I accused Mildred Cosgrove of casting a birth spell. I now withdraw that accusation."

"And the reason for your change of mind?"

"This is a true reading. If I had drawn these cards, I would have made the same prediction. Charlotte's memory convinced me. Mildred is innocent."

Charlotte looked to Tom and James in relief. She nodded and wiped tears from her cheeks.

Agnes turned to the Council. "I'm sorry to have brought the charge. I was foolish." She looked to Charlotte, "I should have asked you what cards were drawn long ago."

Charlotte shook her head.

"Well, I'm sorry all around. I'm glad Mildred never found out." She turned to leave, then she suddenly shot Charlotte a hard look. "Charlotte, Sylvia told me you visited Mildred just yesterday. Did you warn her?"

Charlotte took James from Tom and held him close. "I went to her for herbs. I said nothing of the accusation against her."

"Are you certain?" asked Agnes.

Charlotte looked right at her. "Do you want to search me again?"

"No," Agnes whispered, lowering her head. "No need."

***

At home, Mildred sat at her table. She spread the tarot deck face down before her. She asked, "Outcome?" and chose a card.

167

It was The Magician—a figure standing confident and sure, wielding the arcane symbols of the tarot.

The skillful accomplishment of a goal.

Mildred laughed softly. Good enough, she thought. For today at least.

She poured peppermint tea into her lopsided cup and drank it.

Transcripts of Tapes Found Near The Depot, 06-45

Laura Duerr

Laura Duerr is a speculative fiction writer and social media coordinator from the Pacific Northwest, where she lives with her husband, their rescue dog, and too many cats. Her other stories have appeared in Escape Pod, Shoreline of Infinity, and Gallery of Curiosities.

Tape 1

It used to rain a lot out here. Not as much as some places, but enough that we kinda earned a reputation for it. They would joke that summer didn't officially start until the Fourth of July because before then it would be in the 60s and raining.

The 60s sound downright frigid now. And rain...let's see...it rained last December. Early in the month sometime. It's hard to keep track of dates these days.

It used to be green around here too, green and beautiful. The hills had these huge forests all over them, and the downtown buildings stuck up between them like silver pillars. On those nice, sunny days—you know, the ones you treasured because they were so damn rare, if you can believe it—on those days, the city looked like something out of the future.

Well, the future as we'd hoped it would be. Exactly the opposite of what we got.

I guess I should say why I'm recording this. Power's been out for years, obviously, with the rivers too low to run the dams. Before that we were using the Internet to try to get aid, but it was bad everywhere. There wasn't any aid to send. Around August of the third really bad year, the weather forecasters just quit posting their predictions because there hadn't been any change to predict. All those websites just said "help."

Anyway, some folks had their own generators, so here and there you could get Internet if you needed to know something specific, or if you hadn't yet given up on contacting loved ones. But the news just kept getting worse and worse from all corners of the world. Finally, a year and half ago I suppose, even the folks with generators couldn't get online anymore. The weirdest part was no one seemed to know why. You'd think with all that information that'd been careening around for so many years, we'd be able to figure out why the world had ended, but all we got were wild rumors about aliens and liberals and nukes.

I guess the truly weird part was that we didn't mind not knowing. What difference would it make? Still no water.

Christ, it's hot.

There used to be huge forests out in the mountains between the city and the coast. I haven't been out there to see if they're still standing, but I can guess. I know for a fact the farmland's still out there, both because I can still see it on clear days and because that's where I got run out of.

I haven't thought about those people in a while: maniacs claiming to promote "freedom"—those are finger quotes there, listeners—loaded with crates and crates of ammo and rifles but not enough water to drown a fly. No farming knowledge either. Good riddance. That land must be looking real bad by now. They chased me out nearly two years ago and even then it was turning yellow. Well, some fields are always yellow, but they're still *green*, you know? Still alive.

Oh yeah, the tape. So there's no more Internet, no planes, hardly any cars or trucks...none that can be trusted to transport stuff, anyway. Paper's mostly used up. Still loads of batteries lying around, though, and if they aren't too corroded they mostly still work. I built a converter for my laptop but I save that for when I boot up to look at my old pictures of my grandkids. They were five and two when the bottom fell out of the world. The oldest should've been in high school now if everything...well.

So this tape is my invitation, I guess. I found a whole box of them in a basement so I can record a bunch, put them out here and there, maybe someone will be able to play one.

I've found a good spot up in the hills west of the rail depot. It's small, but the soil does alright, and it's secluded, which I figure is the most important part.

So if you hear this, come out and join me. I have corn, beans, melons, some tasty cacti, even a couple apple trees. What's mine is yours, if you're willing to put up with a cranky old lady made extra cranky by the end times. It's, let's see, early July, 2041.

Oh, and my name's Linda. That's probably important. Look for the blue flag on the split pine. I'll see you soon.

***

Tape 2

It's Linda, again. Or, if this is your first tape: you're tuned in to End-of-the-World Radio and you're listening to Linda!

Christ, that's lame. Sorry. People were barely listening to radio when the world ended, anyway—everyone had all the music they could ever want set up on their phones. My son got mine all...

I—I'm sorry. I don't think about them often, and it kinda—well, grief sneaks up on you, you know?

It's mid-October now and I've been thinking about Halloween and all the ways the world used to honor the dead. Halloween didn't do that hardly at all, but it used to, back when it was Samhain. Even when Day of the Dead got all trendy, most people weren't necessarily in it to celebrate the dead—they just liked the face paint, the sugar skulls. Maybe it was just being in America, or the Northwest, I don't know—we just never liked to reconcile with our deaths, or death in general. When death happened, we liked to push it away, bury it quick and say your prayers and start moving on, because we thought moving on was something we actually could, or should, do. We don't like grief, the way it wells up unexpectedly, the way it sticks in our minds and our chests and won't be forced out. We don't like feeling weak.

My grandchildren...oh, Christ.

I need a minute.

See? That all happened ten years ago and it still stops me in my tracks sometimes. And I can't afford to cry anymore. Waste of water.

I guess the hard part—the part that truly sticks in my heart— is not knowing exactly when it happened. We kept in touch through the slow heating, but then communication got spotty. He said they were going to try to reach Canada, where it might be cooler. How they were going to manage that with a first-grader and a three-year-old, I can only guess.

I daydream that they made it, and that they have a nice little farm, like mine, tucked away somewhere safe and cool. I imagine them jumping in puddles...

Oh, Christ Almighty. I hope they're alive, I really do.

Speaking of farms, though: these tapes are supposed to be invitations, not the diary of an old lady. I get sidetracked, so sorry about that. If you're looking for a safe place, head west from the train depot, up into the hills. Got a nice gully with some food growing, if you're willing to help out. Look for the blue flag on the split pine. I'll see you soon.

***

Tape 3

I used to bike everywhere. The city was famous for being bike-friendly—or at least it was *built* bike-friendly. The drivers could've used a few more lessons. I got hit three times when I was a commuter. Wrecked the bike all three times. Had to get ankle surgery the third time, too. That was right before I retired. I'd planned to stay in the city, but my son made a fuss, so we found me a place in the suburbs. It was nice actually—big lot, big enough to build some planter beds and grow a nice garden. And it was close to the trails, so I could go out there on my bike and not worry about getting taken out by some tech-startup kid zipping around in his electric car. They used to have the most gorgeous trails out here, back when there were forests. It's still pretty, in a way, all the stripped-down gray trunks, but then you remember it's all dead and that kinda takes the beauty out of it.

I saw an old electric car the other day. Totally stripped down. Kind of a shame—the thing could probably still run—but cars are full of useful stuff, so I can't blame them. The seat fabric makes good rain gear. I even lived in a tent made out of taped-together Volkswagen upholstery for a few months. I remember it was Volkswagen because what other company put *plaid* in their vehicles?

Anyway. Oh, the bike. My chain broke and I'm down to my last spare, so if anyone finds these tapes and comes to visit, if you can bring me a bike chain, I've got five liters of filtered water with your name on it. Oh, and I've only got six tapes left, so if you want to keep End-of-the-World Radio Hour with Linda on the air, see if you can find any cassette tapes, too. Say a prayer for Sara W. who found me and stayed here for a few weeks: she brought three tapes and a whole shoebox of batteries, bless her. She said she's heading to Canada, too. I used one of those tapes to record a message for my son and his family and sent it with her. Just in case.

* * *

Tape 4

This is Linda, the blue-flag lady with the homestead. I used to help with the quote-unquote *farmers* out west of the city. You know, the ones with too many guns, no water, and no concept of agricultural practices? This is probably a good time to mention that I took some of those many guns with me when they decided they didn't need an old lady's help anymore.

So if anyone else from the Red Dawners or the Crimson Sunshine or whatever the hell those assholes were calling themselves, wants to come try to take what's mine, when I extended a perfectly polite invitation to come and help, please know that I've gotten pretty damn good with a shotgun.

It's not like there's even that much to take. I told you, I've got a couple of apple trees. Couple means *two*. The Ruby Dawns torched one of them, so congratulations, you complete morons—now we can't have Gala apples anymore. Hope you like Fujis, 'cause that's all that's left.

The corn isn't doing great, either, but that actually isn't their fault. It's August and it's just too damn hot now. Even the watermelon looks unhappy. I don't go outside during the day when I can help it, and when I go out after dark for water, I cover up like I'm crossing the Sahara.

The western sky has been hazy for the last few days, and it's creeping this way. Must be a big fire out there. I told those farmers when I left, I said, if you boys can't quit squabbling over other folks' land and take care of the land you have, you'll lose everything. They were so focused on stealing seeds and saplings from the other settlements, and standing guard over the stuff they'd stolen, that they never bothered to test the soil or monitor the weather or save their damn water.

And the livestock, Christ...the number of people killed over rumors of a new calf or lambs. Rumors. I even said as much: cows ain't gonna give birth in November! But as soon as they heard whisper of someone's livestock doing better than theirs, they'd grab their guns and ride out like they were in a Western. And they'd shoot up the place, then discover I was right and there were no baby livestock to steal. So they'd rope a sad-looking sheep or two and ride back home. And then the sheep would die a couple days later because we barely had water for our own animals.

They never wanted to change. That's how the heating came to happen in the first place: no one wanted to change their ways.

Not that I wanted to change either—I bought local, organic everything, grew my own food when I could, and rode my bike to work, and I thought I'd ticked all the boxes. I'd done my part. I mean, I guess I had, but when the problem's being caused by massive factories all over the world, what's one woman's lifestyle change going to accomplish?

Made me feel better about myself, I guess. That's all. That's all we wanted, then: to make ourselves feel better, never mind how it was making everyone else feel.

Now what remains of the farmlands and wine country is on fire. I don't know what's going to stop it. That fire could be up here in just a couple days, quicker if the wind picks up. I'd say to come visit me, but I may not be here much longer.

Don't know where I'll go. Suppose I could try to see what all the fuss is about Canada.

Before she left, Sara asked me why I wasn't going, if I had family up there. I cracked some joke about adult children needing to get out of the nest already, but really...I know they aren't there. I feel it in my mother's bones: they didn't make it out of those bad early days. I never wanted to go to Canada because I knew the truth would be there, waiting.

If I never go, if I never hear one way or the other...I can still pretend. I can still imagine puddles, and children splashing.

***

Tape 5

The fire's not here yet, but it's close. Christ, the air is bad today. My mother used to tell me about when Mt. Saint Helens erupted and how it rained ash on everyone's house for days afterward. I imagine it looks a bit like that now. My alleys of corn look like the set of a horror film, and the ash-covered stump of the dead apple tree sticks out of the dust like a tombstone. I chopped down that tree and stored the wood that wasn't too charred. I thought maybe I'd smoke some rabbit or squirrel over it, but the fire kept creeping closer and I've just been too distracted by the possibility of having to leave.

It's amazing how much I still had to pack. You'd think surviving the desertification of the world would help you declutter, but I still have too much stuff to carry. Granted, it's all useful—gardening tools and whatnot—but I don't exactly have a Conestoga wagon to haul it in.

And it's been so *dark*. This part of the world used to be so dark and so rainy for so many months at a time that people would actually get depressed from it. Seasonal Affective Disorder, they called it, but I think they mostly made that up so they could use the acronym SAD. It hasn't been this dark in the daytime since... oh, who knows. Since the last good rain. That's how thick the smoke is. It wakes me up coughing.

Shh, hang on! Why am I shushing the tape...

Is it...

Merciful Lord. Ha! Rain! Would you look at that?

I think it's been almost a year since it rained. Oh, I wish you could feel that! I've just got one hand out the door so I can keep recording—can you hear it? Can you hear the patter?—anyway, the drops are hitting my hand and it feels like kisses. It's wonderful.

Okay, it's January 2042, and my farm is still open for business. I've got room for guests, I'm not going to be on fire, and now I'll have enough water to start a new plot. You'll find me west up the hills—oh look, a little creek is forming! Flowing water, I haven't seen that in years—west from the train depot, up in the hills!

Look for the blue flag on the split pine. I'll see you soon!

Death's Armchair by the Sea

Mariah Montoya

Mariah Montoya is a speculative
fiction writer from Idaho. Her work
has appeared in Typehouse Literary
Magazine, Jersey Devil Press,
Metaphorosis, and others.

I am a scumbag of a runner for Death, and not just because I snagged Saint Mary's Nursing Home in downtown Philadelphia as my territory (all runners scoff at us who choose nursing homes; it's cheating they say, but *somebody* has to do it, and hey, I beat all you filthy racers who would have worshipped the gray carpets and old fragile bodies if you had gotten here first).

Here's what happened: Death held a regional conference consisting of a thousand plush armchairs crammed in the abandoned house of a deceased millionaire. Death didn't comment on all the armchairs, but I guessed they were stolen from old ladies who'd relinquished themselves to us in the last generation. Old ladies own the comfiest armchairs, and ours were certainly snug, smelling of stale lotion, mothballs, and prescription meds. I almost felt the human urge to fall asleep—our formless bodies sunk into the velvet or chintz—but then Death coughed politely.

"Thank you all for attending," she said. I say *she* because Death looked rather feminine that day: her scabbed skin swelled over her chest like a reptilian replica of breasts, she wore a burgundy curtain that resembled a dress, and she had grown out strings of flesh-colored hair that brushed the floor. Occasionally, small gobs of oil dripped down her face like melting candle wax.

"Now, this is not a funeral," Death chirped. I was fortunate enough that my armchair was stuffed in the same room so that I could watch a bead of oil creep down her nose. Other runners sat in the chairs that overflowed into the hallway and bathrooms and stairwell, but they could hear through the walls. "It is a retirement party," Death said. "Our dear friend Sheyka has delivered to me seven thousand souls in his career. I release him today to join the natural forces of this world in freedom and honor."

Our murmurs vibrated the floorboards of the house. *Seven thousand?* I had only picked up and comforted and delivered a few hundred homeless souls under the Seattle bridges and in the alleyways of Mississauga, whispering, *If only you let me hold you, beloved Ruth or Larson or Peter or Adya, I can take you home.* And then those darlings (I remember each one) would desert their spirit's futile grip on life and clamber into my arms. If only I could feel dread, I would. Death had never told us what the requisite for retirement was, but if she released her runners based on the number of souls we delivered, then I had a long way to go.

Sheyka, it turned out, was perhaps more of a scumbag than me. I knew so because he morphed his shapeless ass into an almost-solid imitation of John Wayne, grinning and nodding with his chin pointed ceiling-ward at our chorus of congratulations, which made the sky outside rumble with synthetic thunder.

In celebration, Death beckoned a pig from a neighboring ranch, and when the pig came squealing into our parlor, we stomped and clapped and hollered until the poor thing fainted on the Indian rug. The pig was a gift for Sheyka, who was expected to humbly return it to its ranch after the festivities to symbolize the fact that he was not fired. (Over the centuries, runners had passed the irrevocable rumor that the screams of damned souls boiled in the bellies of pigs; if Death fired one of us, rumor went, she would chuck us in the mud for the pigs to eat, and though we could not die, the pig's belly would be inferno.)

After the pig fainting, various runners asked Sheyka, "Wher*ever* did you happen to find so many dying souls?" Each time he would say, "Pardon?" and move on to the next group of runners to talk about toilettes or clothing brands or other trivial matters.

I snooped from my armchair, picking at the frayed fabric. Sheyka refused to acknowledge the repetitive question because, I figured, he was embarrassed by the answer, which meant he had found the souls at a hospital or nursing home. Everyone suspected so, and everyone, including myself, swallowed an internal raging desire to know *which* hospital or nursing home was unoccupied now that the bastard was retiring. We all sat poised, waiting for him to slip up and say the name of some obscure place.

Then I saw an emblem of an eagle stitched into the crease of his John Wayne hat, and I knew from various encounters with cowboyish souls that John Wayne did not typically sew said eagle emblems on his hat. Sheyka–I would've snapped my fingers, had I possessed fingers–was a football fan in Philadelphia.

When the celebration ended with a whirlwind of fake laughs and pumpkin pastries we could not eat, and Death's farewell jingle sang from greasy lips, I did not return to Mississauga–I soared on a hot wind to Philadelphia and sniffed out St. Mary's, where I found my jackpot of dying, departing souls at last: they moaned in beds with white sheets, shuffled to the receptionist to ask when Larry would call, gnawed fried eggs with toothless gums. I would no longer have to pluck children from alleys to fill my monthly quota, and I reveled in this delicious change.

I did not know that St. Mary's would fill me with flesh.

On my first morning, I glided to the nursing home's breakfast hall to search for signs of ailing bodies. I would prefer, I knew, to take souls in bed (oatmeal should never be one's last taste of life), but all good runners take note of their potentials beforehand—who had pneumonia, whose bones might snap, whose arteries were clogged? A few dozen tables stood on a gray-and-darker-gray checkered carpet. A handful of elderlies sat fingering the mush on their plates. I was examining one man with a smatter of liver spots on his neck when I felt a tingle on my own neck (metaphorically speaking, I think). I turned.

A woman sat unaccompanied at a table at the head of the hall, hand trembling as she lifted a mug of peppermint tea to her mouth. Her skin sagged, crusties ringed her tear ducts, and bald spots crowned her head. Her soul was practically peeling off its flesh, but she stared directly at me—yes, *me*—and announced to the room at large, "I'm going to live 'til I'm a hundred and five!"

"We know, Matilda!" the liver-spotted man called. Then he coughed and spat some thick liquid into his napkin. Matilda paid him no attention and continued staring at me. I stared at her. A silent battle ensued, in which I knew the woman should have expired long ago if she could see and communicate with an entity like me.

Don't you take me yet, fucker.

Whoa there, lady.

I'm going to live 'til I'm a hundred and five. I've got three more years.

I can't...you are the deadest person alive, I said. *I have a job, miss.*

Fuck you. It's my personal goal. Haven't you ever had a goal?

Oh yes, I had a goal. I craved retirement. I yearned to escape this dratted job so that I no longer had to taste sad hearts like these.

I could almost feel Death's gaze scuttling across the carpet to my feet, and yes, in that moment, I felt as if I had feet, cold, bare feet with ten toes. Liver Spots coughed again. I braved a step toward Matilda, and another, then another, until I was close enough to absorb her hot, medicated breath. I touched her soul, which quivered like violin strings, or century-old hands holding coffee.

I'll come back for her tomorrow, I said to myself, aware that I was breaking the biggest rule Death had given us: never let a soul persuade. Tomorrow, I said. Tomorrow, tomorrow.

So I whisked away and left Matilda alone and always said, "Tomorrow."

***

Now, don't be fooled. Over the next three years, I obediently ran old souls to Death almost every day, cradling them and singing them lullabies, or Christmas carols, when they requested it. As soon as their bodies stopped pulsing with blood, they recognized me and said something like, "Oh! You came!" or "Why, thank you, I was just wondering how many more times I'd have to brush my teeth." Of course, I ignored Matilda, pretending not to notice the flakes of her soul that fell onto carpet like dandruff at breakfast time. But besides this, I was good, I was good—until Layla.

Layla's husband had departed two decades previously, but now she had a boyfriend, Tom, a hunchback who lived five doors down near the painting of Jesus screwed into the wall. Every afternoon at 4pm, Tom scuffled to Layla's door, knocked, and waited with round, drooping eyes as Layla hoisted herself up from her chair by the window, clutched her walker, and inched toward the door to open it. She never said, "Come in." I usually waited outside with Tom and his sullenness, but sometimes I slipped through the wall (a feat which was becoming increasingly difficult) and gave Layla little motivational speeches I hoped might subconsciously register.

"You've got it, hon! No, don't stop. Keep going. Tom's waiting. *I'm* waiting. Get to the door, that's it. Turn the knob. Yes, the knob. There you go. Yes! You did it, you lovely lady!"

Layla and Tom then made their sluggish way to the chair by the window and the squishy, creaky armchair alongside it (see, old ladies own great armchairs); they hooked pinkies and turned on the news, and Layla would talk about Larry. "Tom," she'd say, "did I tell you about Larry? He's my grandson, you know. He said he's gonna come visit me, Tom! Oh, Tom! Larry's coming! Tom, isn't it wonderful?"

"Nnn," Tom said, mouth agape at the flickering TV. A string of drool trickled from the edge of his mouth to his chin.

"Larry is an engineer. He's very handsome, Tom. He...well, I know he has blonde hair, but it might be black. He loves strawberry shortcake, Tom! I used to make him strawberry shortcake when he was a small boy. He ate his boogers, I think, but that's okay. Oh, Tom! Just think, Larry is coming to visit!"

Larry, I discovered after months of 4pm instances, would never show up; he always promised to visit and discarded this vow the next day. Perhaps I was no different,after all, I was perpetually promising Death that I would soon deliver Matilda,but I sensed poor Layla's soul clinging to her skeleton only so she could see her grandson one more time. So one day, after Layla pulled a photo from her hanky drawer to show Tom, I decided I'd break another one of Death's rules: morphing in front of humans.

I became the Larry in the photo. I was tall with sandy brown hair and an upturned nose and a tiny joke of a thing between my legs. I sauntered to the receptionist desk, scratched my balls, and signed my name in the check-in notebook.

"Room 252," the young man at the counter said, as if I didn't already know. I told him thank you and used the elevator. I rapped on Layla's door. It was 7pm. Tom would have returned to his room to mope and sleep. I waited outside, Tom-less, as Layla fought the aches of her arthritis to cross the room. The knob turned. The door opened.

"Larry! Larry! Larry! *Larry!*"

The woman embraced her grandson after all these years, and I felt the ridges of her spine with physical fingers. My skull throbbed from morphing. I would soon pop back into my ordinary, formless existence, but for now, I carried the grandma to bed, laid her down, and told her stories. My wife was having a baby, I said. No, I don't eat my boogers anymore. I love you too, Grandma. I love you so much. You are beautiful, yes, even at ninety-three. I held her knotted, veiny hands when a nurse bustled into the room to help her swallow tablets and powders. After the nurse left, Layla smiled, closed her eyes, and said, "Larry."

She abandoned her body before the drugs digested, and I carried her gingerly to Death.

***

"I'm going to live 'til I'm a hundred and five!"

"We know, Matilda, dammit, we know!" Liver Spots hollered. It was lunch time. The man was playing Concentration with friends while Matilda sat sipping vegetable soup at the head of the hall. At times, slices of her soul fell off of her carcass like fall-off-the-bone ribs, and I paused watching the game to pick up these pieces and slide them back in place. It was like trying to re-stick old tape onto a wall: each time, the adhesiveness faded, but Matilda would eye me and say soundlessly, *Thank you. I have to make it to a hundred and five.*

You will, Matilda. I'll make sure of it. My chest cramped, and I knew I had crossed some sort of line. The pain was a warning, cold fingers pinching my imagined sinews, reminding me, perhaps, that I had a duty, that I was not human and could not make promises like these.

Sorry I called you a fucker, Matilda said. *I actually like your company.* And, after a moment: *I had to bury my baby when she was twenty-one. I've got to live long enough for both of us. I promised her.*

She resumed slurping soup. Upstairs, a handful of elderlies groaned, wishing to die, but I disregarded this for now (breaking, of course, a third rule of Death's, which sent pain shooting through my joints).

I returned to the card game. I wanted Bart to win today. He was a short stump of a man, with wrinkles carved deep into his dark skin; he always lost memory games, which might have had to do with his dementia. There were only eight cards left and, as always, everyone but he had two or three matches each. So at Bart's turn, as he flipped over a card with a circus clown on its surface, I whispered numbers near his earlobe and watched the goosebumps rise on his neck.

"Two comma one," I said. My breath must have tickled his thoughts, because Bart chose the clown card's twin. He remembered basic algebra, it seemed, though it took a few curses from Liver Spots for him to realize that he had his first match.

A thump from upstairs, one only I could hear. An impatient soul was whacking his nightstand over and over to get my attention. Bart flipped over a toilet-illustrated card.

"One comma two," I said, and Bart obliged, flipping the second toilet card onto the table. Another thump from upstairs, this time louder. It sounded as if a few souls had detached themselves and were crawling to the door, to the stairs, to me. I might have sweated drops of restlessness, but lately the sorrow of losing residents had infused me like nausea.

Bart overturned a glistening image of a cupcake. I willed him to remember on his own – *C'mon, remember, Bart, you can do it. Why can't you just remember? Remember your life* (was I talking to myself?). Bart only stared at the cards, dumbfounded, his interest sliding away.

"Okay, bottom-most left." I only watched for a moment as Bart slammed his second cupcake onto the table, beam stretched wide in triumph when he registered that there were only two cards left, both of which revealed identical, snorting pigs. Liver Spots sighed. Bart hooted through cracked teeth at his first victory. Then, with the image of pigs scorching my eyes, I rushed toward the stairs, where a soul was bouncing down the steps like an angry bowling ball.

I caught the soul, collected the others, and found Death picking mangos in Malaya. She momentarily resembled an old lady with sagging skin, crusted tear ducts, and a bald-patterned head. She squinted at me while I handed over the souls, as if all the rules I'd disregarded were engraved on my face.

"Next time, I'd like to see Matilda," Death said, tossing me a mango for the trip back.

I felt dread. Matilda didn't turn 105 for another month. I had disobeyed Death's commands for so long that it felt as if a cold hand kept molding me into something solid only to puncture me again and again with the ailments of those in St. Mary's. I seared with heartburn, toothaches, diarrhea, fatigue. My misbehavior, it seemed, had peeled away my immaterial existence as a runner, but I didn't fear the pain. I feared the pig. And, by the curious tilt of Death's chin, I knew my end was approaching.

Rule number four: don't break any rules. Or else.

I could not directly disobey Death a final time, so when I made it back to Philadelphia, mango juice trickling down my chin, I asked a nearby runner wafting in a downtrodden neighborhood to take over St. Mary's for a bit. I was taking a break until a friend's birthday, I said. The runner agreed, and I spent the next several weeks watching residents yawn and yap about infants and struggle with digestion and play card games and doze in armchairs.

But mostly, I sat by Matilda, my arms wrapped around her, holding her soul together.

***

On her 105th birthday, the staff at St. Mary's Nursing Home hung purple streamers from the ceiling and ordered a lemon cake for their oldest-ever resident. All the elders still capable of walking or wheeling attended the spectacle, as did various relatives and locals who had seen the party invite in a Philadelphia newsprint. Even a journalist arrived to snap pictures for the paper.

When the breakfast hall was jammed with a hundred hot, living bodies, we erupted into a chorus of "Happy Birthday." I hovered near Matilda as she tried to blow out her many candles. The flames only wobbled. I leaned over her shoulder and puffed for her. When the flames vanished into smoke, the hall rang with applause.

Thanks, chum, Matilda said. *I'm about to piss myself, so take me soon.*

I let her taste the frosting, grin at camera flashes, tear apart all the presents she would never use. Then, though Death was nowhere near, I felt that cold hand at my back, and I could no longer resist my duty. I gathered Matilda into my arms. She snuggled into my chest, humming.

Together, we left the remains of her body, zooming across the countryside to a farmhouse near the Pacific coast, where Death reclined in an armchair by the barn, knitting a pair of baby socks. She was now a youthful woman with tight, creamy skin, supple breasts, and a swollen belly, who smiled at our approach. Salty wind licked my cheeks.

"Thank you," Death said, reaching out for Matilda's soul, kissing her gently.

So long, Matilda. I raised a hand in farewell, fingers numb and blue.

Don't forget to floss, she said cheerfully. And then – *Here I come, baby. I lived for you.*

Death whisked her away, but I remained standing in the whip of the wind, facing the empty armchair, which was white and stainless. The baby socks rested on the topmost cushion. Eventually I lifted the socks and put them under my nose and inhaled the smell of birth.

And now, right now, a pig squeals from beyond the barn.

Here I am. Now you know why I am the scum of the earth, the worst runner, a failure, a rule-breaker, a lover of mortality. I want peppermint tea. I want grandsons. I want birthdays. I'd even take the liver spots and arthritis and pang of missing someone who doesn't quite love you back, all things *no* good runner should wish for, since it's like saying, *I'm unhappy with my job, I wish to die just to verify that I lived.* Surely Death has noted my misconduct and plans to fire me. I should join the pig and let its mud seep into the holes St. Mary's has drilled into me, holes that long to fill with life.

I stand immobile until Death reappears empty-handed. She takes the socks from me with soft, smooth palms. She lifts my chin until we lock eyes, hers a brown whirl of infinite warmth. Then she says, "Would you like a ceremony?"

"Huh?"

"My dear friend, you have brought me nine hundred and one souls in your career. I release you today to join the natural forces of this world in freedom and honor." She puts the socks in her mouth, munches on them, swallows, and winks; a thick, cottony hope rises up my throat, as if I might vomit what Death consumed. I'm not fired? She's offering me retirement? But I have not accomplished what Sheyka did. Weren't numbers the ultimate criteria?

"No," Death says simply. "Now, would you like a ceremony?"

I shake my head. I no longer want to celebrate departure, releasement, finality. Instead, I ask, "Do I go where they go?" *They*, the nine hundred and one souls I have run to Death, the nine hundred and one and me.

"Not yet. You go where they have been. Where you have been

before. Maybe you will appreciate life this time. Maybe, this time, you will choose to love like you love now."

She spreads her arms. I'm disappointed, at first (I want to follow those souls I carried, yes, I want to touch those souls and dance with them and say, Here I am! I never forgot you, see? I never *wanted* to hand you off like a cardboard box in a delivery truck! Here I am, here I am!).

But Death's hands look so comforting. I am, after all, tired. I could slip into sleep.

So I scramble into the open arms, and now I, the cradler, am cradled by Death, who smells of perfume and milk and cinnamon. She carries me to the armchair and rocks me until my eyelids sag, until sweet darkness envelops me, and I cannot open my eyes, and warm walls close around me. The squeals of the pig, the salt, the wind, it all fades...even the tightness of Death's embrace fades, because now maternal flesh tightens in its place, flesh that wraps around me and reminds me of Matilda and Layla and Tom and Burt and all the others who are, if time condensed, both alive and dead, both here and there, both slurping soup and dreaming about Larry. Flesh so mortal, vulnerable, temporary that it hurts.

Blood pulses. Moisture. Voices from beyond a thick wall of meat and fat and skin. Death stitches my soul to a tiny fragile body, kisses me, and departs.

I manage to think, *See you later, boss, Death, mother, friend.*

Then I forget myself. I hiccup. I kick. I squirm in the new womb that holds me.

The Last Evening at Prosperity

Stuti Telidevara

Stuti Telidevara is a twenty-something daydreamer hailing from Bangalore, India, and studies English in the New England cold. Visit her at srtwrites.wordpress.com for updates.

agni

Jaya was late again. The moon was high above her by the time she slipped through the workers' entrance into the bathhouse. She fumbled with her clothes and grabbed a coarse towel from the rack in the cloakroom, wrapping it securely around her waist. "I'm coming!" she said to no one in particular, hurrying into the steam chamber. A bathworker was waiting by the entrance, wearing the telltale green shift. Jaya almost walked right past them before she noticed the tray they were carrying. She let out a long whistle.

"Who let you get at the coffee?" she said, snagging one of the tall, cloudy glasses. Late nights at Prosperity were for employees only, and people like Jaya who never let anyone forget that she had been a bathworker too, thirty-odd years ago. But though the bathworkers were encouraged to use the baths and improve Prosperity's process, they were only allowed the leftovers of the day's food, like rats. Rats did not get coffee like this. The bitter taste struck Jaya hard; she smacked her lips at the sharp chicory.

The bathworker grinned. "The malik's looking the other way for tonight. Might as well, since the likes of us won't use the baths again!"

Jaya tried to hide her grimace. She had told herself to pretend tonight was like any other night, but that was proving difficult. She coughed, and said, "Have you seen Kiren? Short, old-timer like me?"

"In the corner there. Enjoy."

She could just make out Kiren's familiar shape through the billowing steam. As Jaya inched close, Kiren lifted a hand in a halfhearted wave. She was lying flat on her back, limbs akimbo, eyes shut. Jaya could not hold back a snort. She looked so worn down, one would think they were still bathworkers exhausted after the long day. Jaya lay down beside her, taking note of the warmth emanating from her, her fingers flexing—signs of her small-magic at work.

"Knees hurting you again?" said Jaya.

Kiren groaned. "Like fire. I swear they only stop aching when I've been through the Prosperity process about five times. Those bastards are going to keep me in agony if they shut me out of here."

"You have enough magic to treat yourself," Jaya said. She patted Kiren's arm in reassurance, then made a face. Her friend's skin was slick with moisture.

"Well, I wish I didn't have to. I'm going to deplete the bathhouse stores as much as I bloody can before we leave tonight. Lavender scents, please!" Those last words were shouted at the middle of the chamber, where green-shifted bathworkers were barely visible through the mist. Someone cranked the controls, and the air filled with the smell of lavender.

"What does lavender mix well with?" said Kiren. "You think I can get them to add another scent?"

"Oh, stop it. You're only giving them more work to do." The bath-workers were moving in unison, conducting the steam through the room. Jaya focused on the pinprick of awareness in the back of her mind; their small-magic was a faint, happy hum, calling to hers, twisting with heat. She let herself be lulled by the familiar rhythm, pushing away the reminder that it would soon be lost to her forever.

Kiren scoffed. "Work, ha. You think they can get away with mischief when they're on duty during the day? They're enjoying this."

Shapes coalesced in the steam: a snarling tiger, a hissing snake. Jaya frowned. Surely she was imagining things. The first chamber at Prosperity was agni, fire. For people like Kiren, the thick heat was like calling to like, a swirl of energy that heightened emotion so that it could be released in the next room. Jaya's own small-magic had always been a cool, slippery thing that preferred the river's currents to its sunbaked ghats. Even a few minutes in the first chamber felt stifling—made her liable to see things in the mist.

Jaya prodded Kiren's arm. "Let's move on."

"Hay, so soon?" But she sat up slowly, allowing Jaya to help her to her feet. "I'm only doing this because they're serving real food tonight, Jaya. Don't think I'm bending to your will."

Jaya only rolled her eyes. They crossed the warm wooden floor to a set of small doors; the bathworker cracked the doors open so that too much steam would not escape, and the two of them ducked into the next chamber.

***

dharini

They made their way to the raised platform in the middle of the room, dabbing at their damp skin. Thankfully, there was space enough for both of them. Jaya left Kiren stretched out on the hot stone, and went to grab one of the copper vessels at the platform's centre. It was full of a thick green-brown sludge, smelling of herbs and clay and comfort. She hefted up the vessel and brought it back to Kiren, feeling rather proud of her own steadiness. The Prosperity process was taking effect: strength trickled into her tired muscles, and her small-magic stirred like a waking housecat.

Kiren was watching her with an unreadable expression. "What, are you pretending you're still a bathworker?"

Jaya dipped a hand into the clay and began scrubbing it over her arms. "I'm always pretending that."

"Take a washcloth, mu-ma," a voice said. Jaya looked up to see Bo staring at her with definite disapproval, washcloth in hand. Bo's green shift was stained with clay; Jaya had to resist the urge to pull the girl closer and scrape it away.

"Thank you," said Kiren, accepting a washcloth and slathering herself with mud. "Please, Jaya, allow Bo to do her job."

"All right," Jaya muttered.

But the sternness had not faded from Bo's eyes. "You shouldn't be overexerting yourself. Either of you. Who's going to fix your aches and pains after tonight?"

"You," Kiren said cheerfully. "Between the three of us, we can recreate the Prosperity process in the jungle, right?"

Jaya shot her friend a look. "Don't tease."

In the same moment, Bo said, "No, actually, the company's bought the jungle."

"What?" said Jaya, astonished. "What do you mean, bought the jungle?" Kiren looked just as shocked.

Bo glanced between the two of them, and sighed. "Wait here. I'll bring the food."

Something twisted in Jaya's gut. She finished painting the clay over her wrinkled skin in silence. It hardened like a cool shell over her body, helped by the ovenlike warmth of the stone. But it could not shut off her anxiety. Jaya tried to imagine her worries discharging into the earth, like lightning on a stormy monsoon afternoon.

"How could the company buy the jungle? I thought they only bought the bathhouse," Kiren whispered, startling Jaya out of her trance. "Can you...buy land like that? Who sold it to them?"

A hundred possibilities bubbled to Jaya's lips. "I don't know," she said. It was best not to speculate, after all. What good would that do?

Bo arrived soon after, bearing a wooden tray stacked with simple, uncooked fare: flatbread, fluffy cottage cheese, dried figs. She set the food on the stone between them and sat down, folding her legs beneath her. Jaya turned to face her, feeling the clay caked over her skin crack at the motion.

"Eat first," said Bo, offering them the figs. Her small mouth was twisted in unhappiness; her fingers were knotted tightly together. Jaya sensed her magic too, a roiling mass of emotion stirring against its bounds like a river testing a dam. "The company signed a treaty with the shah. They get the bathhouse, the harbour, the whole town. The jungle. All of it."

Kiren waved a chunk of flatbread in the air. "Not likely! The shah was just warring with the company—"

"Times change." Bo's voice broke; she swallowed hard, and looked away. Jaya covered the girl's hand with her own. Bo lived in the strange new way that the company men encouraged—with only her blood family—because her brother had been one of their foot soldiers. At least, before he had died in the war with the shah. Bo understood far more than Jaya did, and Kiren pretended to, about the outsiders and their strange new ways. But the cost was a fractured home, and Jaya could not induce her to join one of the walled communes like the rest of them. Deep in Jaya's belly, her small-magic skittered around like a nervous thing.

"Tell us there's something we can do." Kiren fisted her hands, heat pulsing from her body in waves. "Someone we can fight."

A cold spike of certainty hit Jaya through the warm fog.

"Be silent!" She seized Kiren's wrist with her free hand. "For goodness's sake, Kiren. The malik sleeps upstairs. You think she won't sense something going on here if you spread talk of sedition?"

"It isn't—"

Jaya held up a hand. "Bo, put the tray away. We'll go through to the next chamber." She had no children or grandchildren by her own blood, but Jaya knew that stubborn clench to the young girl's jaw. If she could not draw Bo into her fold, she would have to find some other way to protect her. And the last way to keep any of them safe was treason.

Bo scuttled away, looking still more mulish. Jaya waited until she was beyond hearing to open her mouth again. "You heard her. If her news is true, and the shah has allied with the company, then talking against the outsiders is sedition."

Kiren worked her jaw. "Talk isn't enough."

Now, a real fear curled into Jaya's chest. "What does that mean?"

Kiren met her gaze with a steady stare. "Who is the shah, to barter the land we live on in a treaty to outsiders? Who are the outsiders, to come here on their boats and decide what we do and how we live?"

Jaya knew there were many in town who shared Kiren's views. War had taken a toll on the communes, to say nothing of the factories, which had pulled away those of them with stronger magic. But the outsiders, though they died at a bite of a mosquito, had been clever about this. The powerful were separated, put to work in offices or the company's army, given paper money so that they would stay content. The weak were angry, but they could do nothing about their anger. Jaya would die weak. She did not want to spend the remainder of her life angry.

"Who are we," she said, "to defeat anyone in a fight? You and I have so little magic that we were not even summoned for the factories' most menial jobs. What can small-magic do?"

Kiren had no answer to that.

***

varuna

The bathwater was just warm enough to feel cool after the oppressive heat of the previous two chambers. Here Jaya let her small-magic seep into the air around her, smiled as the scented water swirled into tame little currents. They had scrubbed off the clay and washed off its traces; now they would soak for as long as they liked. Bo returned with their main course, still tight-lipped with some stirring revolution.

"Don't get food in the water," she said, sitting outside the bath and leaning against its bamboo-panelled wall.

"We've worked here same as you, young lady." Kiren popped a fish cutlet into her mouth, letting out a long sound of appreciation. "I hope you won't take that tone with your new, pale-faced customers."

A shadow crossed Bo's face. "I certainly won't."

Sensing that they were coming to dangerous territory again, Jaya took a noisy gulp of the spiced buttermilk. "My, have they improved the recipe for this?" Her attempt at distraction proved useless; both Kiren and Bo ignored her.

"What will you do, then?" Kiren was not teasing anymore, Jaya realised. She was wearing an expression rather like determination. Kiren, who could hardly walk a mile without needing to stop to rest her knees! The comfort of Prosperity was slip-sliding away like an eel from Jaya's grasp.

She glanced at the painted ceiling, picturing the fearsome malik asleep in her silk sheets. The malik kept the bathhouse workers under her thumb with a considerable magic—not great-magic, which was the work of sorcerers, generals, and kings, but not the paltry small-magic that Jaya herself wielded. Even now the malik's magic sat dormant, a faint awareness in the back of Jaya's mind.

What destruction would she wreak on her workers if she discovered what they discussed, between agni and vayu? Jaya was certain now that she had not mistaken the shapes in the steam earlier: a tiger, a snake. Promises of vengeance, symbols of resistance in stories carried from other harbour towns that the outsiders had taken for their own. Sedition eddied in the bathwater, hung thick in the air like condensation. Jaya and Kiren could be overlooked, of course. But what of the girls who worked here every day? Jaya looked to Bo, at the restless push-pull of her magic.

"I'll not take this lying down," said Bo, her voice thick with emotion. "If I must burn down factories to free other magic-workers, I will. The outsiders can't take this away from us."

Jaya shook her head, letting out an incredulous laugh. "Bo, what will you fight with? We have no strength."

Bo did not respond to that, but Kiren gasped.

"What?" Jaya said.

"Speak for yourself!" Kiren extended a shaking hand to Bo, pressed a finger to her collarbone.

There was a sudden flash of light, the sharp smell of something burning—and, far stronger, a dull roar of magic, a surge of power that sent Jaya's small-magic cowering, like a predator's call. How often had Jaya called to another's magic that very same way, to see which little babies in the commune carried it within them? But the responses she had received were whispers in comparison to this. The bathwater sloshed onto the stone floor. Jaya let out a yelp as it turned cold as ice. Every bathworker who had been controlling the Prosperity's fine-tuned process would find their magic stiff with fear.

"Stop that!"

Jaya batted Kiren away, and the force went silent. Warmth seeped back into the water; murmuring to themselves, the bathworkers turned as one to look at Bo. But the greater harm had already been done. Somewhere above, magic sparked up with a start. The malik was awake.

Jaya scrambled out of the bath, dripping water all over the floor.

She fumbled for a towel, and tossed another at Kiren. "Get up. We're going." The last chamber, vayu, would only need a brisk walk. Neither of them felt any particular affinity for the element of air, so there was no need to linger. Jaya was already thinking of the quickest route back to her commune.

But Kiren was paying her no attention. "Great-mage," she said with awe, staring at Bo. "I knew I felt something from you."

"And you had the brilliant idea to test out your theory here! The malik is awake, Kiren. No doubt the whole town felt that." Jaya wrapped the towel around herself, knotting her wet mass of hair at her neck. She called to her fitful magic and drew out the water in a long stream, directing it back into the bath with a flick of her wrist. She could not look as if she'd been here at all. There was no doubt that Bo had kept her magic hidden—and to evade the outsiders' call for powerful magic workers would bring punishment upon them.

"Bo, come with us," said Jaya, holding out her hand. The girl still had not moved an inch since her extraordinary burst of strength. No doubt all the bathworkers would be tested again. Could Bo avoid such an examination? Would the other bathworkers help? Better still for her to be gone before the malik arrived.

None of them even so much as twitched. Jaya grabbed both Kiren and Bo, and pulled them through the doorway.

***

vayu

Bo was shaking her head as Jaya dragged them along. The last chamber was more a corridor, its walls painted in soothing blue whorls that did nothing to calm Jaya now. Little vents brought gentle winds whistling through the hallway, smoothing the last droplets of water from their shoulders. In the middle of the chamber, Bo yanked her arm free.

"I'm not leaving. And let the malik come! She'll take us outside to test us again, and I'll burn down this bathhouse."

Her words held no hint of hesitation. Jaya stepped away from her—from the curling, hot magic she could not keep leashed.

"How could you say that?" Prosperity had kept the townspeople's small-magic in balance for so many years. It was as much a part of Jaya as the salty air, as her own writhing magic. But Bo, she realised, had been born into a different world. A world where outsiders seized the docks and then the young, a world tainted by the seafarers' touch. A girl with power such as hers would not sit back and watch.

Bo's furious gaze confirmed Jaya's fear. "If we can't have the bathhouse, they can't either."

Jaya fought to keep the tremor out of her voice. It seemed to her that they were all three of them on the precipice of something, but only Bo was liable to jump. "And what of the town? The jungle? Will you burn those too, just so the company cannot have them?"

That distant rumble of magic filled Jaya's ears again. "I'll burn everything and start again, mu-ma," Bo said like a promise, "if it means I can keep them out."

Jaya tried to picture that, a town that had not felt the influence of the outsiders. It looked like her childhood. But she knew how they twisted every situation to their advantage, how they fought with the shah one month and signed treaties with him the next. They would be back, like the blight that reshaped itself and attacked crops. Jaya reached for Bo's hand again, squeezing it hard.

"Burn them too," she said. Her voice sounded strange to her own ears, drowned out by the surge of Bo's power. But the girl's grim smile showed that she had heard well enough. Jaya adjusted her towel and hurried through the corridor with Kiren on her heels. They stopped in the cloakroom long enough only to gather their clothes before ducking through the door.

The night air rushed to greet them, the absolute silence punctured only by their gasps.

"What did you say to her?" said Kiren, massaging her knees.

Jaya squinted away from the bathhouse. From here she could see the harbour, still bright with lamps even at this hour, light dancing over the tall sails of the outsiders' ships.

"Nothing," she said. "Come. It's getting late."

Down among the Fireweed

Sarah McGill

Sarah McGill is an author of fantasy short stories, appearing on GigaNotoSaurus and Lyonesse, and rarely ventures past the turn of the century. After all, everything got less interesting after Pepper's Ghost and fugues in silver went out of fashion. She lives in New York City with a kaleidoscope of paper butterflies and a cat who is playing all the angles.

It said upon the gelid gallows, sat down among the fireweed, that Mistress Marjorie Hart was dead. She wasn't hung up from a rope so all peered and read again, and thrice, the words carved on the wood, yellowed as autumn leaves. "What portent's this," they said, "her name writ on the gallows wood when she was recent seen beneath the full-stomached moon like a greying haunt? What mischief and what fairies come and play among the fireweed?" Shook the blue bells and the mad caps beneath the gallows jawing trap so all were to the road and none look back.

***

A fortnight before Marjorie Hart's name was written on the gallows' wood, in dusk and wind-blown rain, Jack Withall came up the road, long into his cups. He'd wept all through the wood, so the river ran behind and his heels rusted through. His mother had that morning starved and died and sent him reeling from the door. He'd not washed her skin or closed her eyes but held his arms against his ears and sunk far away into the wood when the funeral men went by.

Winter-born, Jack had been, and hungry, so that his mother cried and ground the barley flour on a stone. No wheat, no meat, no summer herb kept company with shelf or drawer. No milk beaded on her breast. But rather Jack supped on birthing blood and starved until the dusk. Up the way, Tom Scratch came to play a ditty at the hatched and crossed roads of Carrick town. At the door he tipped his hat to ma'am and redded babe. To her he said, "I'll make a bargain with you. I'll keep you on past Morrow Night with rye, milk, and mutton. In return I'll bind your babe to that grey gate of death, grown o'er with grass and o'er with rush. Hained, he will be a crossing man to part the doors when there is need."

So mother agreed and took his sun-stamped coin. This was done upon Slag hill so at the age of twelve Jack was strung by rusted chain, wrists raw and one eye down the hoary road.

Twelve he'd been, and now a man, his breath of hops and clove, and heavy hung his arms with chains that rattled on death's key-holes like tumbling stones.

At Marjorie Hart's hearth, burnt orange as sear field, he threw his hands into her lap that she might unbind him from his chains or elsewise cut from him his wrists.

Marjorie bent, hand over arm, eyes of silent field and blowing leaves. "You are half-threshed, half-plowed, wheat stalk broken at the hip and left to rot, your fate weaves from rotted fingers." She took a shawl late made of beaten flax and strung it through a widow's ring, like a body through a cloven gate. "A passing through the door, when lock is begun to turn, left eye to road and right still on home."

Jack felt so pulled, stuck between, before and after, twisting away from left to right. But he said, wry, "You make me as a pitiable stone."

She laughed, screeching and moorish, which had earned her

name of witch before her roof was fully raised. "No stone before has been known so much to moan or keep me such good company."

Jack pulled his thumb beneath his eye. "I am only taken so well when compared to such silent companions as your own."

"Well." Her cheeks folded upon themselves beneath her grin. "Perhaps it is so."

Marjorie kept before her door a loamy shovel above a rusted cage and for the town of Carrick dug the musci graves. Like landed sailor, she swung her arms and hips and sang a lover's song: *The magpie's in the water skeel, too late the soldier comes heel to heel.* Some said from her open sleeve she spilled goat's milk upon the graves and so nursed the dead to sleep and not a ghost or haunt bothered the split streets. Others said Marjorie bound fox teeth into the departed mouths and in the night put ear to grave for rumors of their sorrowing.

She tapped her palm upon his shoulder. "I'm sorry, Jack, to hear this morning's news."

Jack shook his head, sunk further elbow to knee. "My mother sent me to Slag hill when I was twelve. I went through old Tom's barley field in the smell of greenish spring, following the rabbit tracks. The dew set upon my toes, the lasted yellow fading off the grass. And away, among the naked trees, the deer wore garlands of horn, hung with red ribboned velvet. Atop the hill I found broken glass cut through my heel."

She held her hands to splayed knees, a head above him. "What such glass?" she said, not unkind. "A witching glass?"

"A naked glass, to catch me in. To steal my eye away." He passed his hand before his left eye, cold and blue, and saw not the chain along his wrist, but the low-slung dead taking deathly road in fireweed and rain. "I sat atop the hill and wept onto my bloodied heel. I thought I was to die, the blood came so thick and fast. A ribboned road I left from field to crown, my first, my own, a terror unfurled off my grief. But I was deceived, as a child is by those who seem to know the world by virtue of certainty and weathered face. I stood at the gate o'ergrown with rush and saw the hoary road; I stumbled and am stumbling still, stepping between, looking back and before. Bound and kept and weaved. Marjorie," he put his hands beneath his knees and so hid the manacle and chain, "I don't want to die."

Again she laughed. "Oh, true? An uncommon thing, no doubt."

He scowled. "You are kith with the dead. With milky tea you picnic on the graves. In yellow summer you lay on fresh-turned soil and weave spells among the broad-leafed trees. At muggy dusk, you skin rabbits upon your knee, the fur left on the head, as a reprieve to digging graves."

"You think I carry barrows in my womb, that I have made to love, to lie, upon death's frozen bones because I know its bed?"

Jack turned his wrists about each other, knotting himself tight to not be furthered pulled through the widow's ring. "You spangle your house with graves, rank poppy on your breast. With rush lantern light and trader's coin you pull the dead upon your door. I have, it seems, seen you put hand through earth and reach to rot-ted hand of those that have passed the threshold and walk west."

Marjorie took hold of the chain between his wrists and made as if to haul him to his feet. "And you are master of death's gate."

He pulled away. "I am no master."

"You are a sullen swain." She served up soup and sat before

him eye to eye. She put her hand beneath his own upon the iron stain and callous wrist. "Jack, for you I have made thistle tea and creams and salves and will again. But I am at heart no hearth-witch, to comfort with warmth after rain and the familiar smell of home."

With quivering breast he took in her somber eye. "If you would have me go, take these chains."

"I am loath to break your bargain."

"It was not I, sunk in dusky loam, who made it."

"It is yours to own, unsightly though it is." She took a bowl of soup to set between her knees. "I was once cleaved from death. I made a bargain and cast the gate behind."

"Then cleave me too! So that we can roam us both to greener place."

Marjorie shook her head. "I bargained for ten years of life, took the sun-stamped coin, and I was quick to regret that piece of gold. I would rather now with soiled hands clothe the dying fox so that we two might die together. I would say prayer to its bones and teach its pounding heart to grow with horehound, to plant heather in its lungs."

Jack bent to his soup and muttered, "The old wives say, when grain rots before its sewn and chickens are slain a dozen in their coops, that Marjorie Hart has gone marrying Tom Scratch beneath the gallows' wood."

Marjorie smiled, bemused. "And your own rumors, Jack, the man of waning moon? The boy upon the hill bound up in chain. Are you not unhallow too?" From her palm she brushed dried rabbit blood and Jack turned away least it show the rabbit's death.

"Jack," she said, "why did you not come to see your mother in her grave?"

He rested his cheek to the hollow of his wrist and would not speak of it, but rather pressed his palm to his blue eye so that it pulsed with night.

Marjorie stood to make a yarrow tea to ease the swelling in his joints. "I once bargained my hide from between the hound's teeth, as your mother did. I would not abide the sight of bone. I now take lessons from the hare's fading eye and the fox's cracking jaw. I unweave."

Jack did not hear. He knew only that she was all that could untether him from his inbetween, of left eye blue on rime and snow and right eye brown of seeded soil and growing wheat.

"We will visit her grave," Marjorie said. "The soil is fresh-turned and in want of care."

Jack did not go, but lay a while beside her fire drinking yarrow tea before he went back along the road all low and sore, bloodied about the wrists.

On the hastened way home to Carrick among the pine, he met Tom Scratch, sawing at his fiddle with an old hen bone and a strangled hare at his waist. It seemed-oh horror-that for a moment with both left and right Jack saw the hoary road and hastened dead barefoot in the snow. Until from his pocket Tom took a pair of dark-pipped dice.

"I do not play," he told Tom then, when offered the first throw. Feeling as bare as an empty loom, he said, "To bed I keep my bones when deals are made. I take no interest in their gleeful cries."

"Be you priest or be you brother, to speak such lies?"

"I am neither, be on your way."

"Will you sit and listen to me play?"

Down he came onto a mossy stone, wrists bound and bent, chain-handed and moon-hooked. He watched Tom play at *Bones in the Pot*, horsehair and catgut bending to crossroad chord. Across his teeth it split, and upon his tongue he tasted cordgrass wet with rot and camellia winter-deep. The stars sunk down, unclothed and bright, of bluish midnight light and lozenge on the wind.

Jack was tossed between the stag's branched horns that pierce the swollen moon and spill milk like blood across a stony vein. He turned on dark-glass eyes as of the deer that stood among the misted wood and were lost among the trees. By left and right, by in-between, by done undone and unmade sain.

Jack lifted hand and offered palm. "Will you these chains unlatch?"

Tom Scratch put arm to moon, woven bands upon his wrist of hemp and skin of sheep. "Will I unbind what I have bound? Will I leave the gate, which is surely not my own, but gift to all, unmanned? Would I? Tom Scratch? You are moon-caught, lad, her reaping scythe set into your breast and her waning eye beneath your chest. Hein, you stand in thrall, lost between life's road and ours."

How tired Jack grew then and he ceded all thoughts of comfort or of steaming cup. He knew, in truth, it was a foolish thing to ask. Tom Scratch could not break his own bargain. "I'm home then to my bower."

"Well, not so fast, after all, I am Tom Scratch. Though late the hour I might find some answer with stave and rue."

"And what must I give to you?"

Tom shook a careless, but expectant, hand. "I will bargain your chains against your life's end. That once they are broke, I will gain the choosing of your death."

"And bargain breath?" Jack held his face. He didn't know how Tom would cleave his own deal, but he didn't think it mattered. "Yes."

Tom Scratch grinned all of teeth, and when he flipped a coin from thumb to air, Jack was the fool to catch it.

***

The night before Marjorie Hart's name was written on the gallows' wood, she stood upon her threshold, stew gone cold and winter on her back. Tom Scratch sat before her fire; broth wicked down his chin as he sucked meat from rabbit bone. Behind her she could feel the fox and hare bound o'er the field, in hunt and play, and turned toward death.

Tom'd not hung his coat at the door, but kept it at his waist. It was of amber-red like baying hound and spun of warp and weft so sometimes Marjorie saw thickets strewn of mongrel track and brambles full of frozen seed.

Tom turned up a scalded eye of rimy blue. "Hard cold tonight. The rabbit's to its den, the mouse beneath the leaves."

Marjorie nodded to frost and hoary moon.

"A body's like to freeze. Blood gone black and bones nigh cracked."

Marjorie gathered fox hide to her shoulders and smelled musty pine. "The moon's turned scythe, reaping brittle sheaves."

Tom frowned and hunched around his bowl, slunk with baleful eye. "The sleepless left to grieve."

"Is it true? Ten years are past and made the hound's catch?" Marjorie felt those ten years slipped, lost among the drifts of snow and fallen pine. She slipped herself and desired more, another spring creased with lovat clouds and sudden rain.

Tom turned broken bone between his teeth, his face of sickle and blasted wheat. "Caught, and bargained to Tom Scratch. The apple's frozen from its stems, figs and almonds grown from hand-sown seed." He took his fiddle from its seat and plucked a tawny string. "Time is up and a bargain must be paid."

Marjorie sunk her hands into the fox's hide, felt the growing wood, the spring that would come soon with Mallow Night. She pulled down her heels so she'd not show her fright. "You have no dice to throw? No second bargain to rattle my bones?"

Tom raised a delighted brow and put thumb to chin. "No."

Marjorie grew cold.

Tom set down his bowl. "So, it is my half of the bargain, to choose your path after you die. After death you will turn astray from hoary road and go without eyes–pricked by needle and devoured by flies–until you are led by sun-stamped coin to proper death among the rue."

"My own?"

Tom stood and from her mantle took the coin he'd ten years past put into her palm. "That is already used."

Marjorie watched him turn the coin between his fingers and wished she had her leather cap close at hand, that she might take a final turn about the field. She would soon enough lose her away among loosened meadow, to mourn, to haunt. And perhaps there was no other coin, no wayfarer possessing the sun's face that could open death's gate. She nodded to Tom farewell.

Tom grinned and she was snared in net of forest pine; set before snarling hound with upcurled lip. The wind chilled of bone and the fire flickered cold. Dim it grew, so shadows danced that cut eye from eye and mouth in twain, crossroads set on moon-scythed lip. Marjorie drew closed her loamy hands and she was clothed in death—by fox and hare and bear—lost among the fireweed.

***

On the day Marjorie Hart's name was written on the gallows' wood, Jack came with click and kick in shoes of iron heel and holly on his hat. With wrenish fright he took the news from the folk of Carrick town that Marjorie's name was writ onto the gallows' wood. Omen, it seemed, evil and strange. He bobbed his head and flushed bright red.

"Not I," said he. "I'd do no such dreadful thing. Nor was I called to open the gate o'ergrown. Yestereve the locks were all made fast and the window's open wide. I heard no calling in the night of death, nor whistling wren or hawking craw, and slept until the morning's light." Tight he pulled his coat around his sagging chest and clicked his heels so he'd not sink through rime and frozen earth and set his mind on that long hoary road that in the ground lead west.

"We'll go," Jack said, "and call to Mistress Hart from the field so at the window she can show her face." And to desperation he slipped as hands were into pockets turned.

All looked to road that at the edge of town wended like a tattered sheet. It went among the pines and through the watchful shadows that turned on travelers late at night. Grey, it was, and green as lichen and ice caught among oak roots. On it went by den of black-eyed hare to Slag hill where in the lee Marjorie skinned her meat.

"Gristle and gall," the ale's wife said, "I'll not turn to the hill like gallows maid, as if my grave tax had been this morning paid. I'm as like to from a fairy's basket take cheese and mead for this eve's sup."

So Jack imagined Marjorie beneath the drying sage, beating bone to bone. Slat of hip and rib, drummed on her own hide, stretched and dried, so fox and hare throb and run where bones lie under leaves. And all the dead beat in time with rotted hearts.

Kith and kin drew closed and listened for death's mortal tryst, the crash of gate, the drumbeat cleaved from sound. Jack stood, left eye shut in dread. He feared her death, to see it twisted round his eye, to pierce him like a briar thorn.

"It is a jest," Jack cried, "that the young boys have played upon the gallows wood. I will go myself and call to Marjorie Hart from the field and find her putting lilac on her breast."

All bit lips and put unfriendly eye to Jack's rusted chains, so he went alone to that unhallowed road. By vixen den and, hung from pine, fairy homes made by children's hand on Morrow Night. By blighted ash grown with pulpy blue and bleeding stone where beer and mead was thrown. Past where the road was made of rock and silence sat among the woad.

Marjorie was all of hunt and grave and flint, Jack thought. She'd not be dead. Who else would keep his right eye open, to look to boiling iron pot and hedge gates grown with rain-dark mint? To the fallow field Jack came and turned his heels around, so he looked down on Marjorie's berth and saw her shovel gone from its perch. Moorish wind, albicant and cold, turned his coat tails over and he pulled his arms tight.

"Mistress Hart," he called, his feet among the fireweed. "Marjorie."

All was still and the lantern was unhung from Marjorie's fence, but rather laid among the grass all broken glass and cooling wax. A blueish rain began that bent the stalks and leaves. Jack put hand above his hollyed hat and didn't knock, but pushed inside to Marjorie's berth to keep his body dry.

He breathed musk, Marjorie's rafters swung with fox pelt and hare. Charcoal burned dark red and damp, unstirred. When he set wood onto the hearth, the stifled smell of gutted creatures grew. Under the grey light and the rushing sound of rain, he saw her upon the frosted ground among the uncured meat and anise seed. Marjorie Hart was, rightly, surely, gone. Already, from her chest red heather grew, rooted in the lung, and horehound in her heart. About her hips like pelvic bones nested barrow moths and bulbous flies on her skinless knees.

Jack took down his hat and it trembled at his breast. "No cock nor crow came to laud your departure in the night."

He crouched before the dark fire and came apart; from himself he spilled like red seeds from a jar.

"Marjorie." Jack wiped his cheeks. "I've not the heart to bring you to death's gate. I've not the way through lilac field, having spent these last dozen years straining against blue death, my wish to pluck my left eye out. You need make your own way to the hoary road."

The moths took up, like leaves and wind, and settled down, as if in augury. "If you'll not take me," she said, "I'll not go."

He started from her corpse. "How's it you speak?"

The light took up her face, skull full exposed beneath her shriveled eye. "By trade and pay. By the sun-stamped coin you took when the night turned bleak."

"Your name is writ on gallows wood."

"And I will go. But take me on. I hear your chains that run from skin to bone, all along the hoary road."

"I will take you if you would but set your foot onto those frosted chains that through the keyhole runs like sateen scarf through widow's ring, and break them both in twain."

"You would ask that now?"

He clasped his hands and his palms were chilled. "Please."

She might have taken then his arms so he would feel how her hands trembled in fright, but what flesh remained was stiff and he did not reach for her. "You were given blight of boon. What fool deal did you make? Was it not enough to be bound once? Think you the second will break the first and not cut straight through your spine?"

"He found me on the road. I am blown as if into a ditch."

"He cast it thus," she said. "Jack, listen close. Listen here. Tom cannot break your bargain. So he would that I crack your chains across my knee. He knew you would ask it of me in return for leading me to the hoary road. Then Tom may take what he would in payment for orchestrating this plan. And you will be the worse if that is done."

Jack beat his heels and turned away. "No other will come to your door, should I go."

Marjorie's voice rose. "It is because of you I stand among the fireweed, blind to the frozen gate, o'ergrown with grass and reed."

Jack listened to the beating rain, his final chance for reprieve slipping away.

"And I must pay a crossing tax, like a hare that must skin itself for the hound, when I have done you favor of keeping you from turning both eyes to the hoary road and losing sight of green? I have propped you like a mother against my knee and this you will not do? Would you not even keen for me or sing lament, but rather rapine my rabbit bones and funeral pall, as I may no longer raise cry and hue for thief?"

Jack gripped his wrists and the skin was stiff and blood showed through above the knobby bone. "You will not help?" he said, all hushed.

The moths stepped across each other's backs and made a confused path across her bones. They'd lost their way, it seemed, and walked, blinded, over their sisters' wings.

Jack thought to touch her palm, gone wet and blue, but he startled from the morbid skin and could not look onto the bones appearing from her peeling shin. "I sink down into the graves," he said, "and the dead lie upon me chest to chest and hands clasped, as lovers do. They would put their mouths atop of mine so that I am as of unwilling lover. I was not bound to grave but married, married and tied by ring and veil so that I must not just watch the flesh rot, bled from red to blue, but love and let it down my throat.

"I know that you speak to the dead, that you have held them

hand to hand. You have taken sorrows from their mouths and bound them among the drying sheaves."

Marjorie scoffed, as of flapping moth wings. "In recompense for a bargain I never should have made. So that I would not loath the dead as I once did."

Jack dropped his head and put bloodied wrist to eye.

The mayflies buzzed harsh and fast, blue-bottle bodied with glassy wings. The red heather bent and swayed, as on a forgotten grave. "It is a terrible thing, to wander," she said. "The hay's gone gray, the sheaves undone. I walk on frosted grass and cannot see the trees." The horehound, bittersweet and clung with musk, bent thick and sorrowful leaves. "Did you look on your mother when you found her dead?"

"As a death-bound son made prey. As a shackled child sent early to such a hard apprenticeship."

"You did not look?"

He shook his wrists and felt his eyes grow wet. "My bargain is made."

"Take me on," Marjorie said, "so that sun-stamped coin can't be drawn further along your hand. A flail that flays you to the bone."

"Then go yourself. It is a well-trod road."

The moths turned in circles.

"If you will not," Jack dropped his hands, "I will take the knife from your drawer and part my wrists at your door."

Rain dripped from the rafters.

"You are a selfish man."

The rain blew open the door and wet the entranceway, so it sunk into grey and shallow pool. The mayflies walked down Marjorie's legs and the bone showed through.

"Give me the widow's ring. I will unbind you from the gate."

"Marjorie."

The moth's silenced the humming of their wings.

"Marjorie."

But she said no more.

The water spread across the floor, spattering his ankles. Jack put silver ring, black with age, into her palm. He laced her boots. The moths and mayflies bloomed to the rafters, leaving her bones bare. His tongue failed, twisted stump, dead root. There was more–a keen, a ribbon around her waist, the room swept clean–but he did none. He looked through his left eye and reached and opened death's gate. The rain blew against his back and the moths flew out. When he saw her step onto the hoary road, the chains from death's keyholes bowed around her ankles and drew up through her widow's ring. They snapped and fell about his feet. The shock sent Jack's wrists numb.

He heard then such a booming sound, so great, like howling beast, like yowl that sent foxes to their bellies with their tongue about their teeth. And when he took his last look, before death was struck from his blue eye, he saw the gates barred full closed and not, again, to open to the sound of his iron-heeled shoes. Locked, weaved as he unweaved.

Out the window he saw Tom Scratch, digging Marjorie Hart's grave.

He walked into the rain and took the lantern from the grass, shaking from it the broken glass. Cried the jackdaw from its hedge and leapt the hare from juniper bush. The hare bound over yellowed field and into rimy sky, greying quick with rain. Tom set the shovel into the ground. In his hands he gathered from the graveside poppies and rain-rotted briar sheaves. Water dripped from his hat and he mocked sorrow with rimy eyes.

Jack felt the fool. "Scratch."

Tom held forth the damp bouquet. "It looks she got away. On to noble death, a bargain paid." He shrugged and his smile cracked Jack through. Tom chuckled, light, wheat beard against the wind. "What shall I play?"

"I could not say."

So Tom played a ballad, *Down Among the Fireweed*, and laughed when they parted ways, red-bellied hound baying from the gallows wood.

***

They call him Jack-a-None, age to age, the story passed mouth to mouth along the fiddler's bow. He wanders down the evening road with his lantern held full high. It bobs and drifts and always runs from coffins rested on shoulders in funeral parades. It is said when the night is hazy and the moon is shy, he calls out to a wild-witch, to cleave the deal she made with him. That she would hang him from a gallows and open up the trap. For he has lost the way to death, cannot find the gate o'ergrown or hoary road. He goes undying and alone. But she doesn't come and the lantern turns, weeping in the dark, through rimy fields and grasses white with frost, fog clinging to his back.

Bog Witch

Maya Dworsky

Maya Dworsky is a PhD student at the
Brandeis University Anthropology
Brandeis University Anthropology
Department as well as a Fellow at
the Schusterman Center for Israel
Studies. She has often sought both
escape and insight in the worlds
of fantasy and science fiction, and
believes that the endless potential of
imagined Other subjectivities holds
the key to our survival as a species.

Taterra had not been left on this world.

She had not been banished, or forgotten. She had not been sent away in disgrace or in punishment, or as some form of cosmic torture conducted by a childlike and petty-minded deity.

Taterra had chosen to be here, on this horrible backwards moon, and she reminded herself of this fact at least three times a day. Sometimes more on days when the weather turned swampy, and her joints swelled, muffled electricity hummed between the clouds of insects, and the lakeshore became indecisive about its role.

Days like today. When the air hung weighted down with wet and sparkled in the last of the sunlight, clinging to Taterra's flesh and hair as she set up her fishing pole at the end of the dock. Creaking and groaning, she leaned back in the folding chair, and perspired.

Trust Charles to send her somewhere where climate control was still a distant, sweaty fever dream.

Taterra had not joined the Lioness Project as a young woman. She had been well into her sixties when Charles, the smarmy bastard, had begun frequenting the last-row seats of her lecture halls, inviting her to dinner parties with fellow wealthy nut-jobs. When she came, he attempted to lay claim to 'our dear Dr. Mystic.'

"Oh, silly me," she could hear his smooth, well-oiled laugh rever-berate off omnitemporal cocktail glasses. "I do believe it's pro-nounced *Myshtaq*. Yes, she's doing some *marvelous* work for us in ecological crypto-ethnology. Wrote the book on it, in fact. Such a star, our girl."

Taterra was not his girl. She was not anyone's girl; Taterra had tenure.

But Charles was indeed the star around which the rest of them—those few biologists, linguists, and other scientists he'd managed to gather from far and wide—orbited suspiciously. Charles and his distinguished, silvery temples. His long, slender hands, and weathered skin. So much squinting at the slopes leaves such fine, fine marks.

The thought of those slopes now, from her current sweltering position, was almost cruel. Like the memory of delectable flavor on a starving man's tongue.

Taterra had signed on to the Lioness Project after only two week-ends at his ski-lodge. Even in her darkest moments, trapped as she was on this barbarous mudball of a moon, surrounded by savages, she couldn't bring herself to regret it. Even knee-deep in nettles and malaria, in a place that felt like punishment, she couldn't have possibly imagined the volume and quality of data she was collecting here.

She'd been skeptical when she'd first heard of it—the idea of a long-lost settler colony striking her as more of a sensational-ist novelty than a research opportunity. She'd laughed at him, pouring herself another glass of Argentinian Malbec, then hissing as a few drops landed on the Egyptian cotton sheets. "You can't expect me to believe you found a true first-contact society, Charles. Or should I call you Captain Cook?"

It was the second weekend and he already knew he had her. They both did.

He'd reached past her and pressed one long brown finger to the new stain, and they both watched as miniscule beads budded out of the fabric. He'd swiftly gathered them, and placed the finger in his mouth, sighing at her. "Not first-contact, my good doctor, never first. But first in a very long while. Hecate III was a prison moon, well over twenty generations off the grid. Barely Bronze Age, from the satellite data."

"You've bought yourself a satellite, have you?"

"I've bought myself a moon."

"Whom from?" She'd finished off the wine and ran the inside of her wrist across her lips, leaving behind the very last traces of lipstick and sediment.

He'd rolled his sharp, dark eyes, and bright teeth flashed in a laugh. "What does it matter, Tati? A penitentiary conglomerate, if you must know. An old one. What matters is that these people have been living untouched, *pure*, in a dark little corner of the galaxy, and I'm handing them right to you."

She'd watched him for a few moments, her eyes narrowed, her mouth tight—she could feel the parenthetical lines that cupped her lips, the lasting acidity of the wine fizzing brightly against her gums.

"And do you intend to go full Leahy Brothers on this dark little corner? Kill the natives for their riches and brand yourself the Cortés of a new era?"

"There are no natives, darling," he'd sighed at her. "And there are no riches. There are... possibilities. Likelihoods."

And that was the first time he'd told her about the family. The elite who called themselves Men of Hu—the descendants of a divine lineage, marked by their white hair, who ruled over the rest of the populace like the fairytale kings of old.

It was the first time he'd told her of the *magic* they claimed to have.

She'd looked at him, skeptical. "Excuse me?" Taterra had spent her life as a social scientist, and as such was inclined to accept more nonsense than the average whitecoat... but there was a limit even to an anthropologist's credulity.

"Their language isn't complicated, shouldn't take you more than a few months to pick up," he'd continued, ignoring her, reaching over to fiddle playfully with the edge of one grey curl that draped over her shoulder. She'd worn her hair long then.

Taterra had flicked his hand away and sat up, gathering the sheet around her. "Charles,"

"Yes, Dr. Mystic?"

She'd narrowed her eyes at him. "What are you looking for."

He'd leaned in close, grinned brightly, and whispered, "*Magic*".

"Charles, it isn't magic if you understand how it works—"

"Hear me out, Tati." He had cupped her jaw in one of his large hands. "Imagine studying this family and the people who believe in them—they say every firstborn is male, and has hair as white as snow—"

"Genetic probabilities—"

"*Imagine,*" he'd pleaded. "Imagine if it were true. If these people created their realities, if their beliefs shaped the laws of physics, of genetics, of *probability*. Imagine a world where ideology shaped existence rather than the other way round. Where there is nothing either good or bad, but thinking makes it so." A cheerier, more self-satisfied Hamlet had never spoken.

She'd watched him for a few moments, then sighed. "What are the study parameters?"

He'd tried to hide his excitement, but couldn't. "They are yours to set, Tati."

"But what am I trying to *prove*, Charles?" Then she'd realized how far she'd allowed herself to be carried. "What am I saying? There isn't an ethics board in the galaxy that'll grant you approval. We could never design a study that—"

"What ethics board?" His eyes had gone wide, innocent, his mouth small and quivering like that of a child amused by their own attempt at dishonesty.

Realization had dawned on her slowly. "Charles, does anyone know there is a living colony on Hecate III?"

"The natives call it *Yereyoch*, apparently. It means Green World, or Green Moon or something of the sort—"

"Who knows there's a living colony on Hecate III?"

"Everyone who needs to." He'd waved her cares away, the light glinting off his long, manicured nails. "Remember, my good doctor, this project is entirely self-funded—you would operate in the name of none but yourself. Design, execute, analyze the work independently. Answer to no one. No peer reviewers, no red tape—"

"I get it." She'd cut him off, keeping down the swelling in her chest that threatened to burst forth as hysterical laughter. "And what do you expect me to do, exactly?"

"Insinuate yourself into the royal family," he'd whispered, moving in for a kiss she knew would taste of wine and smugness. "Become the bog witch I know you are."

And that was indeed what Taterra had done.

They had droplanded her here in the dead of night, and she had slogged her way through these swamps for the very first time, carrying with her only enough tech to make the moon survivable for her, and for theatrical necessities.

Taterra had made her way to the castle built from ancient prisonships, and performed for the king. He was a tall, blue-eyed, copper-skinned, white-haired man with a stern face and a credulous heart. He loved to watch the lights dance, unaware of the imagers tucked into the depths of her sleeves. She had a ritual—she would touch each long-nailed finger to her thumb in turn, and then, hands splayed, she would perform wonders for the king and his court. She could see and show sights as yet unseen.

The king, patriarchal and cruel but far from stupid, had kept her on as illusionist and wisewoman. This gave her opportunity to befriend the young queen. Wide-eyed and sweet-tempered, the little girl taught her the lore of the land as she had learned it herself. Or was learning it presently, young as she was.

The white hair was known as the Mark of Galad, symbol of the

HuMan King. For as long as anyone could remember, the king and his rightful heir had been known to their people by this mark; it had been passed down from father to son for generations.

"Never to a female heir?" Taterra had asked, as she and the queen—a tall, willowy, umber-toned girl of ten, still too young to conceive but old enough to wive—paced through the gardens one morning. "There's never been a daughter born with the right to rule?"

Never. The concept was entirely foreign. Over the years, however, Taterra had managed to convince the queen, as well as many of the other court women, that this was a thing not only possible, but inevitable.

The court women had spread it to the chambermaids, and they to the farmers' and fishermen's wives and daughters who delivered food to the castle. It wasn't long before the thought had cemented itself in the minds of the populace: the next Prince of Hu would be no man of woman born. But a woman herself.

It had been prophesied by the witch. By the very pricking of her thumbs.

The king raged, threatened to banish the witch back to the bog from whence she'd come, but Taterra had assured him these were only silly rumors and that she had made no such prophecy. His son would surely come to him in time, he need only wait. She calmed him with illusions—lovely lights and music painted with her fingers across the air of the courtyard. She made pretty pictures dance for him, and made him feel big in the knowledge that her alleged power was his to command.

Still, the whispers persisted. They twisted, changing from one teller to another, buffeted this way and that like wind over the rising heat of the swamp. A female child would be born, taking another's life as her own.

When the queen was quickened, the baby within her turned. Breach came and the queen-child was lost, even as the queen's child lived. Taterra mourned her, but celebrated the birth of the little prince.

The queen's last act in life was to name her daughter Bartholomew.

The king's rage was spectacular. Not only was his firstborn son a daughter, but she bore the Mark of Galad—by all accounts, she was the Prince of Hu, rightful ruler and heir to his throne.

Not bad for a mere decade's work, if Taterra did say so herself.

And yes, the king had banished her back to this horrible swamp, and no longer called for her during feasts to make the lights dance, but the little girl prince was growing stronger and smarter by the day, and would come to her—sneak away from the prison castle to see the bog witch, the woman who had foretold her coming.

Bartholomew loved Taterra, listened to her in all things, allowed her mind to be shaped by the witch's words and stories. Taterra was excited to see the kind of *Yereyoch* she would make. How it would change around her like the center of a kaleidoscope.

The sun had set over the bog witch, and Taterra blinked in the blue darkness, her fishing line still untroubled. With little thought but a slight wince, she brought arthritic fingers to thumb over the water, and lights began to dance over the surface.

Very soon, the fish were biting.

Once, she'd had to use tech to fool an idiot king into believing she could conjure lights from thin air—now all she needed was to think it, and the lights appeared. Enough people—courtiers, farmers, and their wives—believed her to be capable of magic, and so she was.

Charles had been right. The people here shaped their world—the building blocks of their reality were comprised of belief. Of magic. Charles had been right to imagine a world where ideology could change, and with it, existence.

It was a shame he'd never see it.

He had handed her a moon, a world, in which nothing ever happened but thinking and believing made it so. Which meant that—should it be believed—anything could happen. Taterra intended to conduct her own study, her own set of experiments. If there truly was magic in the universe, it seemed that she had found it. And moreover, she understood how it worked.

Dr. Taterra Myshtaq stood, reeling in the last of her catch. Looking back over her shoulder, she saw that the HuMan Prince had come early, and lit the lanterns. Gathering her things, the bog witch started towards the cabin she'd built with her own two liver-spotted hands, and smiled at the sight of yellow light breathing in the windows.

Thank You To
Our Supporters

Many thanks to our patrons and supporters, especially:

**Anna O'Brien • Cathrin Hagey • S Naomi Scott
Natalie Weizenbaum • Siobhan Beeman**

**Emily Anderson • Felicia OSullivan • Kennon Hulett
Katherine Montalto • Shannon White
J'nae Spano • Martin Cohen • Salomao Becker
Shelly Jones • Tessa N • Tory Hoke**

**Jocelyn Actual • Carly Racklin • GriffinFire
Isabel Cañas • Jen G • Kayla • Liz Warner
Maria Haskins • Suzanne Thackston**

Want to see your name here? Become a patron!
patreon.com/lunastation

About the Cover Artist

Eran Fowler is an American illustrator currently living in BC, Canada, who graduated from the Alberta College of Art and Design with a BDES in 2010. Eran has always been interested in the storytelling possibilities of visual art, and feels most at home using magical realism to explore what it means to be human.

Eran has worked both in-studio and as a freelancer. They continue to look for more opportunities to learn and grow as an artist.

You can find more of their work at:

eranfowler.com

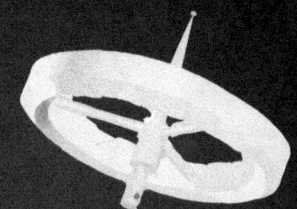

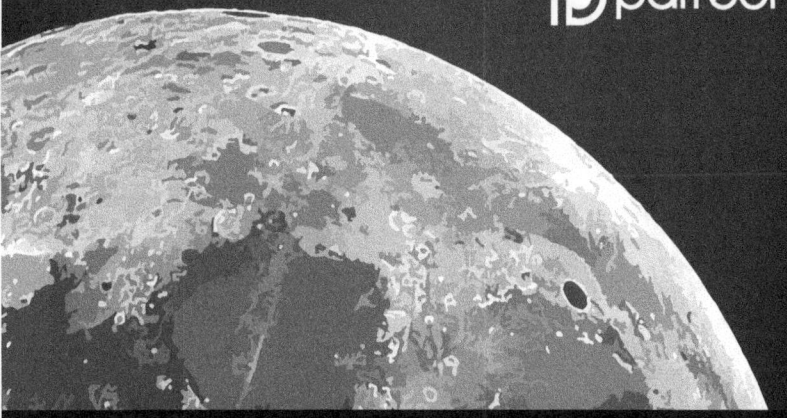